W9-CXP-726

SABINA

SABINA

A Story of the Amish

HELEN R. MARTIN

BARNES & NOBLE

NEW YORK

Originally published in 1905

This 2009 edition published by Barnes & Noble, Inc.

All rights reserved. No part of this publication may be reproduced,
stored in a retrieval system, or transmitted, in any form or by any means,
electronic, mechanical, photocopying, recording, or otherwise,
without prior written permission from the publisher.

Barnes & Noble, Inc.
122 Fifth Avenue
New York, NY 10011

ISBN: 978-1-4351-2051-8

Printed and bound in the United States of America

1 3 5 7 9 10 8 6 4 2

CONTENTS

PREFACE

THE PSYCHIC PHENOMENON DESCRIBED IN THIS story is not fictitious; the writer can vouch for the truth of it.

For some of her facts about the Amish the writer is indebted to Mr. William H. Richardson, author of a pamphlet entitled *The Picturesque Quality of the Pennsylvania-German: An Address Presented at the Eleventh Annual Meeting of the Pennsylvania-German Society.*

Sabina

CHAPTER ONE

THE WILTS HEAR STARTLING NEWS

THE WILT HOUSEHOLD WAS IN A STATE OF excitement bordering upon consternation. Levi, the head of the family, had just come in from the barn to the large kitchen, where his wife and children, together with Susanna, his wife's widowed sister, who lived with them in the capacity of "hired girl," were all gathered about the dinner table; and the announcement he had made as he took his seat had almost the effect of a dynamite bomb.

"In town there at market this morning, I tole a young man where [who] ast me, that he had dare to come out here to our farm to board with us over August. He'll be out here till four o'clock this after. He comes with the trolla-car or the stage to New Holland; then I got to hitch up and fetch him from New Holland out."

"But, och, Levi!" gasped his gentle-voiced wife, Naomi, as she paused, dumfounded, in her task of putting "spreadin's" on a huge slice of bread for her little daughter Melinda, "we ain't never took no boarders! And a *city* person yet! *We* can't board no town young man—and us an *Amish* family! We're too common, Levi!"

"And a party we don't know nothin' about!" cried Aunt Susanna Wilt, whose predominant characteristic was a morbid tendency to scent calamity. "Now, mind, Levi, but you're gettin' yourself in a trap! You don't know *what* fur kind of people it has in the world!"

The followers of the Amish faith do not live "in the world," their religion, by its unique customs, and the peculiar garb it imposes, setting them apart from the rest of humanity, prohibiting "a life of vanity," and rigidly enforcing a plain and frugal manner of life and conversation.

The Wilts, seated about the table in the clean but most plainly furnished kitchen, that served also as the family livingroom, would have presented a strange appearance to an uninitiated observer. The two daughters, Sabina, a blooming girl of eighteen, and her little sister Melinda, aged six, were dressed exactly like their mother and aunt, in the Amish garb. They all wore white caps and bright green frocks of cheap merino, made with a straight plain skirt and a tight plain waist; and over this a black merino apron.

Levi's two sons, Aaron, a young man of twenty, and Samuel, a boy of eight, were also the exact counterpart in dress of their father. They wore trousers cut alike behind and before, vests fastened with hooks and eyes (the Amish faith forbidding the worldliness of buttons and buttonholes), and dark-brown shirts, all of cheapest material. All three were in their shirtsleeves.

But the most remarkable point in the male attire was the fashion of the hair, the Amish creed prescribing a bang to the eyebrows and flowing locks behind, reaching almost to the coat collar. This curious cut of the hair, together with the mild and serious expression of his countenance, gave Levi, in common with many of his brethren in the faith, a remarkable resemblance to the conventional pictures of Jesus; while the face of Naomi, his wife, was strikingly suggestive of the Botticelli type— fine-featured, pure, and childlike. The parents looked very little older than their grown-up children. With the exception of Aunt Susanna's alert expression and bright mouse-like eyes, the countenances of all the family indicated a sleepy and apathetic existence.

The table, as well as those who sat about it, had its peculiarities: there were two dishes of everything—potatoes, cabbage, stewed "snitz" (dried apples), stewed dried corn, platters of fried ham, and plates of bread cut in mammoth slices; there were at least four kinds of "spreadin's," or jellies, on the table, and three kinds of pie. The idea in this Amish table-custom of duplicating every dish is that the food may be within reach of everyone, so that, the necessity of handing things to one another being dispensed with, undivided attention may be given to the business in hand of staving off starvation. Each one cut his own piece of pie with his own knife.

"But, Levi," his wife asked almost tearfully, "what made you think fur to do it? Just to think of a stranger city person comin' to live with us a whole month!"

"Well, it was this here way," Levi explained, with his habitual placidity, quite unmoved by the sensation which his news had caused. "The young feller come up to my market-stall in there at Lancaster, and he ast me was I Mr. Wilt. 'That's what some folks calls me,' I says. 'But I'm Levi Wilt. Us Amish we don't favor the wain language of the world.' 'Well, Levi,' he says, 'do you want a summer boarder?' 'I ain't never thought about it,' I says. 'What would you

be willin' to pay now?' 'What would you want?'
he ast. I studied a while, and I says, then, three
dollars a week. He says that would suit *him* all
right. 'Who are you?' I ast him, 'and what do
you want with comin' to our place to board?'
And he says he's a artist where makes pictures
that way. 'Do you keep such a photygrap gallery?' I ast; but he says no, he ain't one of them
fellers; he draws his pictures. 'That ain't so easy
done, say not?' I ast him; but he says it comes
right handy to him. He wants to draw some
skeens out here near our farm, and board with
us about a month, he says. I spoke that there
Scripture to him where it says make no likeness
of anything in earth or heaven. Well, I had him
there—he couldn't come over that there. He
didn't answer me nothin'. . . . . He's comin' till
four o'clock a'ready."

"But how do you know," Aunt Susanna suspi-
ciously asked, "that he *is* such a artist where he
says? He might mebbe be a sharper!"

"I can tell a good bit by guess. He looks it so.
It's plain at him that he's one of these here
drawin' fellers. He has such a pointy beard and
his hair is near as long as us Amish weare ourn."

"What fur lookin' man is he?" half shyly inquired
Sabina, the eldest daughter—endearingly called
"Biney" by her kin—speaking for the first time

since the exciting subject had been broached. She raised her brown eyes to her father's placid face.

The sound of the girl's voice produced a peculiar effect upon the assembled family. Instantly a silence fell upon them, and every eye was fixed upon her with a sort of strained attention. There was nothing in her simple question to account for such a reception of it. It was not the question, but the fact that it was Sabina who spoke, that focused all eyes upon her.

The girl had a strange face—one that, unlike all the rest of her family, suggested an uncommon individuality. There was a deep, strange light in her eyes, quite unexplainable in combination with their lack of bright intelligence, a clairvoyant look that was uncanny. Her face was wistful, almost discontented, as though a very blind soul reached out gropingly for something beyond the deadly monotonous experiences of her farm life. She was pretty and, like her mother, gentle and very feminine. Yet there was a droop to the mouth which indicated that she might have been fretful had such a temper been allowed to manifest itself in this well-regulated Amish household. Levi, the father, mild as he appeared, ruled his family in quite the old patriarchal fashion; and his strict though gentle discipline extended even to his fair eldest daughter, upon whom he, no less than all the other members of the household, looked with a certain superstitious awe. This attitude of mind toward the girl was manifest, now, in the father's altered voice as he addressed her, and in the tense faces of all those who listened, though the reason for it was not at once evident.

"Well, so much as I know, Biney," he answered, "he's young-lookin' and wonderful clean. He has such white cuffs and collars on hisself, and his hands look like as if he never worked nothin'. He wears such eyeglasses, and he has a wonderful big head of black hairs and such a pointy beard to him."

The latter items might have suggested a wild man from Borneo or a goat, but the family accepted them without consternation.

"How had he heerd about you, pop, that he ast you was you Mr. Wilt?" Sabina asked.

Her voice, like her eyes, had an indefinable quality that thrilled one with its marvelous sweetness. Yet, strangely enough, it was not wholly pleasing. Why, it would have been hard to say. Perhaps because it suggested, like her eyes, a mystery in the girl's character, an uncanny something that chilled even as it fascinated.

"Well, that there I ast him, too," answered her father, "how did he hear of me. He sayed he just went to every market-stall and ast fur board, and Ezra Zook's they tole him mebbe Levi Wilt's would take him, seein' they had a plenty of rooms at their house and kep' a hired girl and had a growed daughter to help with the work. . . . It'll be makin' a little, too, Naomi— three dollars a week."

"He must have money—to be spendin' like that all summer without workin' nothin'," said Aaron, wonderingly.

It might have seemed from these remarks that the Wilts were poor. On the contrary, Levi Wilt was one of the richest Amish farmers of Lancaster County, owning his farm "clear" and having a comfortable bank account. But to any Pennsylvania German, and more especially to a frugal Amishman, a man must appear a plutocrat who could "lay off" from earning money while he "spent out" what he had. Moreover, an Amishman is never too rich to lose his keen scent for small profits.

"Aaron!" his Aunt Susanna said warningly, as she lifted a great platter and helped herself to a piece of fried ham, "you'll have to look after your girl pretty good, with a *town* feller hangin' round to make her unsatisfied with *you!* Girls is so easy led away with the pride of the eye!"

"Elephena ain't so foolish like some," Aaron said, with a faint uneasiness in his voice.

"She is in the world, so she ain't held back, like Biney, from choosin' her steady company where she wants!" insisted this prognosticator of ill. "Biney's steady company, Ulmer Popple, he ain't no need to watch *Biney:* she wouldn't do like you—run with a party where's not a member of meetin'. You'll mebbe have need to watch Elephena good, Aaron! Yes," she sighed, quoting one of her favorite proverbs: "'Happy who is single yet, sad who is engaged.'"

"I ain't watchin' her," quietly returned Aaron, whose mildness, unlike his father's, had a touch of effeminacy, strangely coupled with an unconquerable obstinacy. "It's good if she sees other ones before she chooses. Ulmer Popple's the one has need to watch out!" he added, lifting his heavy-lidded dark eyes to his sister's face and smiling, though his tone was serious: "Biney don't never seem to care if he comes or stays!"

Biney's eyes were fixed on her plate, and she did not look up or answer.

"If this here stranger has got more money than you'll have, Aaron, till your pop's deceased," Aunt Susanna insisted gloomily, "Elephena's mom'll favor him, and Elephena she's so 'fraid to spite her mom, she'd mebbe take him instead of you, if he ast her—fur all she liked you better. Elephena she can't never stand up fur herself against her mom. And her mom she don't like us anyways, because Elephena would have to turn Amish before she could marry you—unlest you wanted to lose all you'd get when your pop's passed away; fur your pop's too consistent a Amishman to inherit goods to a son where married out of meetin'. There ain't no consistent Amishman would do that, Aaron, and you know it. You wouldn't do it yourself if *you* had a son where married out of meetin'."

Aaron did not reply, but he knew well enough that his aunt spoke the inexorable truth. In all his life he had never known but one Amishman to choose a mate outside their own fold. It was as unusual an occurrence as for a white man to marry an African. Therefore Aaron's devotion to Elephena Schwenkfelders, a Lutheran, had caused consternation among all his kith and kin. It was, however, taken for granted that he would not marry the girl unless she gave up her false church of the world and came into the true gospel faith of the Amish.

"I'm afraid we can't suit this here stranger," sighed Naomi. "And then how we talk still! Everybody here talkin' Dutch; we ain't never round the English, and so we bring it so hindforemost out—and he'll mebbe laugh at us onct!"

"Never you mind, Naomi," Levi retorted. "His laughin' won't hurt the three dollars a week we'll be gettin' in."

Levi was devoted to his gentle-voiced Naomi, treating her with as much tenderness as she, in her turn, cared for her infant children. He thought her the best and sweetest woman in the world, and in their simple way they had always been serenely happy together. She deferred to him in everything; and any wish of his, even to the least detail of their domestic economy, was a law to her, as indeed it was to all the household.

"Well, Levi"—Naomi resigned herself with a sigh to the inevitable—"I hope it'll turn out all right. But I feel wonderful oneasy!"

She glanced with furtive wistfulness at Sabina. The girl's youthful color had faded from her cheeks, leaving them very pale; and her eyes of mystery seemed to look beyond and above those about her, as though she were only half conscious of their presence.

"Biney!" her mother said in a puzzled tone, "are you—"

Levi turned his big cow-like orbs upon his wife. "Leave her be!" he ordered.

Sabina did not appear to hear either of them. The subject was dropped; but from time to time one after another stole a furtive glance at her. And thus the meal progressed in uncomfortable silence.

Levi and Aaron rose presently and went out to their work; and soon all the others had separated to their heavy household tasks.

As Sabina washed the dishes in the "out kitchen," the conflicting emotions of her mind bewildered her, even as her bearing and expression had bewildered her family at the table. Never before had she been confronted with such an anomalous mental impression as that which had come to her during the discussion of the expected stranger. She knew that she was distinctly glad he was coming—glad of such diversion in her dull, monotonous existence; glad that the new and wonderful experience would be hers of seeing at close range a being of "the world"—the world of which she knew naught save that her religion forbade all contact with it. And Sabina knew, though she did not formulate the thought, that she was glad the stranger was a young man.

But in conflict with these pleasant expectations, there was a dark shadow in the background of her consciousness, vague, elusive, and quite unlike the vivid, startling forewarnings of evil that had come to her on several former occasions. So faint, so shadowy was this image of dread today that she could not clearly grasp it at all, or read into it any sharp significance. Yet it was there persistently, tormentingly; marring her anticipation of agreeable diversion, stealing the color from her cheeks, making her heart turn cold with an indefinable fear even while she was thrilled with unwonted gladness.

She tried to ignore it, as she fixed her thoughts upon the weighty problem of how to devise some excuse for putting on her "other frock" against the arrival of the strange young man. She was conscious of a vague sense of shame in her wish to look her best before him, and not for the world would she have betrayed this wish to her family.

"I'll tell pop I feel fur ridin' in town with him when he goes to fetch out the boarder—*then* I kin put on my other frock," was her subtle solution of the problem.

Later, when there came a little respite in her afternoon's work, she went out to the field where her father and Aaron were digging potatoes.

"Pop, have I dare to go to New Holland?" she asked timidly. "I ain't been on the buggy fur so long a'ready, I feel fur a little ride onct."

Her father rested on his hoe for an instant and looked affectionately on his comely daughter.

"All right. If mom says yes. It makes me no difference."

"There's Ulmer!" Aaron announced suddenly, and the other two, following his glance, saw a white canvas-covered wagon coming down the road toward the potato-field. "What does Ulmer do, Biney, ridin' out Saturday afternoon yet?" Aaron wondered.

"I don't know no more'n you, till he tells us onct," said Sabina, who always half resented any assumption on the part of her family that she and Ulmer Popple were "as good as promised." To be sure, Sabina knew that if Ulmer could have his way they *would* be "promised." But she had never been able to bring herself to speak the final irrevocable "yes," in spite of the fact that Ulmer was the best matrimonial prize of all the Amishmen of her acquaintance, that she was the envy of all the girls who attended meeting because of his preference for her, and that her parents strongly desired the match. This reticence on Sabina's part was not due alone to the Amish custom of keeping an engagement a profound secret—even, if possible, from the immediate families of the two lovers—until a week before the wedding, when it is "published" at meeting. Sabina herself scarcely understood her own repugnance to a definite agreement with Ulmer.

As for Ulmer, he could not bring himself to take seriously her slowness to accept an offer which he knew any Amish girl must regard as a mighty good one—seeing how well off he was; how big and strong; and what good morals he had! In his self-esteem he attributed to shyness Biney's apparent want of appreciation of what others rated so high. Indeed, Ulmer had rather a strong contempt for "the female sek," so abjectly were his feminine acquaintances wont to take his snubbing of their amorous advances. All of them, that is, except Biney. Ulmer could not understand why she should take so much pains to try to appear indifferent to him—he was confident, of course, that she was not really so—and sometimes her coolness so angered and annoyed him that he would punish her (cruelly, as he thought) by going off and "keeping company" for a few months with some other girl. But he never kept that up very long. Biney was very alluring. And she, too, would be well off when her father's ample possessions were divided among his children. Then, too, her very indifference and the difficulty of his wooing were, unconsciously to himself, spurs to his ardor.

Ulmer was rather an exception to the average mild and gentle-spirited Amishman in his tendency to conceit, his proneness to brag of his wealth and to domineer. But he was, withal, a well-meaning lad.

There was that about Biney—a mysterious, unexplainable something—which sometimes put a temporary check upon his ardor; but this was rare and always very temporary. Ulmer was, on the whole, both constant and loyal.

"Well, Biney," he called as he drew up to the fence in his white-topped surrey, a style of wagon peculiar to Amishmen, "I got to drive to New Holland over. Come and ride with. Have you got the time?"

His appearance, as to the cut of his hair and his clothing, was exactly like that of Levi and Aaron; he was in his shirtsleeves, and wore an enormously broad-brimmed hat, the conventional headgear of an Amishman, in shape like that of an English curate, but much larger.

"I—can't go—in this here frock," faltered Sabina. She did not want to go with Ulmer at all. Her heart was quite set upon going with her father; but the situation presented difficulties.

"That there frock's all right," Ulmer affirmed, scanning his lady's green-clad figure. The question of dress is an exceedingly minor one to the

Amish, since all their clothes are cut after one pattern, the only variety being one of color; the most uncompromising shades of lurid purples, greens, and blues are favored. Sabina had worn this same bright green frock often in driving with Ulmer, and why should she make that an excuse for not driving with him today?

"This is my workin'-frock—I'd have to put on my purple," the girl insisted. "And I wouldn't keep you waitin', Ulmer."

"Oh, I got time a-plenty."

"I don't want to go along," she said with a pout. "I don't feel fur ridin' in the middle of the afternoon yet, when the sun's so hot. I'd sooner go with you, pop, after while," she added, turning to Levi.

"Come, come, Biney; you better go with Ulmer."

"I don't feel fur goin' with him, pop," she pleaded; she was afraid her father would command her to go, and that would leave her no choice.

"Well, Ulmer"—Levi turned to the chagrined lover—"I ain't forcin' her any. You and her must settle them things between yourselfs, still. You better learn her to mind you now, or you'll never learn her after you're married. I don't know what makes her act so ugly."

"Biney," Ulmer demanded, looking both puzzled and displeased, "is it that you're spited at me fur somethin'?"

"No, it ain't nothin' like that, Ulmer," she answered. "I just don't feel fur it."

"All right," he said stiffly. "Come on, Dolly," he addressed his horse, pulling on the lines. "I'll give yous good-by, then," he added, glancing toward Aaron and Levi and ignoring Sabina in the salutation.

"Ulmer!" Sabina took a step nearer the road.

"Well?" Ulmer checked the horse.

Sabina spoke to him in lowered tones as her father and Aaron resumed their work.

"I'm sorry I don't feel fur goin' with."

Ulmer did not answer, but pulled again on the reins. "Come up, Dolly."

"Ulmer! When will you be comin' over, then?"

"I don' know."

"Are you spited at me?"

"You might as well come along, Biney."

"I don't feel fur it, Ulmer."

"All right," he coldly returned, gazing over her head. "There's them as would be glad to go."

"Go and get 'em, then," retorted Sabina.

"You'd be sorry enough if I did!" Ulmer snapped at her.

"If you feel fur goin' to keep comp'ny with another girl, Ulmer Popple, *I'd* never try to keep you."

"Well, I *don't* feel fur goin' with no other girl. I tried a many a'ready, and you're the only one I didn't get tired of till I'd run with 'em a couple months."

Sabina looked down and pouted. Her mouth was wonderfully pretty when she pouted.

"Ach, Biney," Ulmer coaxed her, feeling a longing to kiss the sullen lips in spite of his chagrin, "come on and go with! Ain't you will?"

"Ulmer, not today."

"You're a wonderful set girl, Biney. Well," he said resignedly, flapping his reins on Dolly's back, "if you won't, you *won't*, I guess."

"Good-by, Ulmer."

"Good-by," he answered, in a tone of discouragement, as he rode away.

Aaron stooped to pick up a stone and tossed it out of the field into the road. "I never could see, Biney," he said, leaning on the fence, "why you wasn't more satisfied with Ulmer. You might be glad you got the chanct to get him! And what's the use of your thinkin' you kin make up to a person that's of the world?"

"I never did try to make up to *no* man, Aaron!" Sabina quickly answered, a touch of pride in her soft voice. "And I ain't never goin' to, neither. And *you* ain't got no need to talk about making up to a person in the world—look at Elephena! A Lutheran yet!"

"But I'll join her to our meeting if we get married," Aaron answered, a faint red dyeing his forehead, and his sleepy eyes shining softly.

"Her mom won't never leave her do it!"

"Me and her ain't asting her mom dare she."

"Elephena's wonderful afraid of her mom," Sabina persisted.

Aaron's over-sweet countenance took on a look of obstinacy which seemed to promise deadly defeat to Elephena's "mom," as, abruptly dropping the discussion with his sister, he took up his hoe.

"Aaron!"

The brother paused in his work.

"Aaron," she repeated, and there was distress and sympathy in her face and voice as she spoke, "you mind what I tole you onct, how when you speaked to me that you and Elephena was gettin' married some day, I seen—the Face! You'd mebbe ought to give her up and choose another one, Aaron!"

Aaron looked vaguely troubled, but he did not falter. "Even that ain't movin' me any, Biney. I'm goin' to have Elephena, an' if I die fur it."

"But s'posin' *she* dies fur it, Aaron?"

"I'm goin' to marry Elephena," Aaron repeated.

Sabina turned away and walked slowly back to the house.

CHAPTER TWO

The Arrival of the Artist

THE VERY GENTLEMANLY APPEARANCE OF MR. Augustus Acker was in such marked contrast to that of the inhabitants of New Holland that he was the object of curious attention from the loungers about the hotel while he waited for the arrival of his Amish host who was to take him out to the farm which was to be his home for the month of August. He was the subject, also, of excited speculation on the part of the landlord's two young daughters, who, peeping from behind a window shade, watched him as he leisurely paced back and forth the length of the porch that surrounded three sides of the old stone inn. But Acker, absorbed in his own meditations, remained unconscious of the sensation he caused.

Levi Wilt's statement to his family that it was "plain at him he's a artist" did, rather graphically, describe the young man, with his Van Dyck beard, wavy brown hair, and all the other concomitants of the type. Yet there was no affectation in his get-up. His features were strong; his eyes and forehead bore the stamp of keen intelligence; he was well built and muscular; he looked scholarly and interesting, and his whole appearance and bearing were those of a cultured man of the world. There was a peculiar charm in the odd combination of humor and gravity in his face; for while his eyes seemed to reflect an earnest and spiritual side to his nature, the curve of his rather full lips suggested a decided sense of humor.

The broad fields stretching out from the village to the foot of the distant hills, the clear blue sky overhead, and the fresh, sweet country air, made the young artist feel that he had done well in electing to spend a month in this neighborhood.

"It's an unknown world into which I'm venturing," he mused as he realized how little he knew about these Amish people—nothing, indeed, except that their queer appearance at the Lancaster markets had impressed him as indicating a very remarkable peasant type, the men handsome and well formed, with almost a Grecian regularity of feature, and the women so

pensive-looking, they made him think of caged
animals transported to an alien clime. He was
possessed of a desire to know them in their
native surroundings, to learn what was the religion and what the life that had produced these
odd people—and then to use his knowledge in
some art work which, whatever else its characteristic, would at least be unique in theme.

He was scarcely conscious of the underlying
motive which had led him to seek board with
the family of Levi Wilt. In walking through the
Lancaster city market-house one morning, his
eye had chanced to fall upon the face of an
Amish maiden behind her father's stall, and he
had been instantly arrested by the remarkable
expression of the young girl's very beautiful
eyes—an expression so unusual, so inexplicable,
that as long as he dared do so he had lingered
near and watched her. This had been nearly six
months ago, but the expression of those mysterious eyes had not faded from his mind. It had
haunted him persistently, demanding a solution. So, though not fully conscious himself of
the fact, it was this little Amish maid that had
lured him to her father's farm.

A canvas-covered wagon presently drew up to
the inn, and Levi Wilt got out, leaving Biney
concealed in the back seat.

"Can you wait just a minute while I write a postal card?" Acker asked when he and his host had exchanged a brief greeting. "I forgot to ask you this morning for your post office address, and I want to send it to Lancaster at once to my friends. Can we drive by the New Holland post office on our way to the farm?"

"The New Holland post office is just across the street down there a piece of way," answered Levi, as he gave his address.

Acker sat down on the porch bench, and scribbled a few sentences on a card.

"Now I'm ready," he announced.

"You kin write wonderful fast," said Levi, holding out his hand for the card. "It takes *me* longer'n that to write off such a postal card. I'll take it over fur you—I got to go over and get our *Weekly Intelligencer.*"

Acker hesitated an instant, fearing that when he reached the post office Levi might succumb to the temptation to read what he had written.

But he was not prepared for the frank interest in his affairs which his host at once manifested; for Levi deliberately stood before him and read the card aloud.

My long-haired friend of the hooks and eyes and his canvas-covered chariot are waiting while I

write this, so I can't say more at present than ask
you to forward my mail, please, to New Holland,
Lancaster County, Pennsylvania, care of Levi
Wilt. Levi, by the way, is a very promising sub-
ject for investigation. Write to me.

Yours,
A. A.

Levi made no comment, but turned away and walked across the street.

Acker, after a moment's mental anguish, as he stood waiting on the porch, resigned himself, characteristically, to the inevitable.

"If I'm refused a lodging in this vast wilderness, I can only take the next car back to Lancaster—and the joke will be on me!"

But when, a moment later, Levi came back, his expressionless face bore no indication of anger or offense. Acker did not, however, feel wholly reassured.

When he climbed into the wagon he was suddenly brought face to face with Sabina.

"I make you acquainted with my daughter Biney," said Levi, stowing away the stranger's luggage in the back of the wagon, and gathering up the reins.

Acker lifted his hat and offered his hand in cordial greeting. He was not a little startled at this unlooked-for and sudden contact with the object of his curiosity and speculation.

Biney shyly held out her red, work-roughened hand and let it be clasped in Acker's long, white, nervous fingers, her young face, framed in its ugly purple sunbonnet, flushing with self-consciousness.

Acker had a swift impression of gentle dark eyes meeting his in shy interest, but in whose shadowy depths lurked an expression that was hauntingly strange and uncanny.

"I took notice to what you wrote on that there card," remarked Wilt as they started down the road; and Acker set his teeth to meet what might be coming; "that you called me Levi. Well, that there's my name. I don't favor bein' spoke to like what you spoke on market this morning, callin' me Mr. Wilt. And our childern ain't never heerd no one called 'Mister,' so if you don't mind, we'll leave 'em call you by your first name—unlest you'd sooner they'd say 'Uncle'; all the strangers they have saw yet is relations to 'em. You see, us Amish we don't never travel with other ones. Us we stick to each other. What is your first name, anyhow—and do you mind if we call you so?"

"Not in the least," Acker hastened to assure him, relieved that he had given no offense.

"They may call me what you wish. My name is Augustus."

"'Gustus,'" Levi repeated experimentally. "You hear, Biney?" her father turned to instruct her. "His name's 'Gustus."

"'Gustus," Biney repeated in a low voice.

"I understand," said Acker, turning in his seat to include Sabina in the conversation, "that the Amish of the county are nearly all related to one another—practically one family—because of the intermarriages growing out of the prohibition to wed outside your own sect."

"Yes; I don't know no Amishman where ain't married to his cousin," Levi admitted. "Some thinks that ain't good fur the risin' generation. But I never took notice as it made nothin'."

"The Amish whom one sees at the Lancaster markets," Acker admitted, "are certainly robust, healthy-looking specimens of humanity. But there is a remarkable sameness of type among them."

"You think?" Levi's tone was uninterested. Such speculation was too subtle for him. "The reason we marry our cousins so much is that we like to stick close to each other and form Amish settlements, still. We try to make farmers of all our sons and give 'em farms near us when they get married, so they don't move away. To keep 'em satisfied to be farmers, we darsent leave 'em get too much educated, so we just send 'em to the district school a while, and that has to do 'em."

"And of course you must keep your daughters uneducated, too, or they would not be willing to marry the farmers—is that your principle?"

"Yes, them's our ways. You wrote on that there postal card," he suddenly resumed, "about our 'chariot.' That there's some fancy a name fur such a old wagon like what this is. It's hardly safe to ride in no more. Sometimes I think it'll all fall together yet! I'm stoppin', on the way out, at Israel Baer's carriage shop to get my new carriage where I ordered made. I hope," he added dubiously, "it won't be too proud-lookin'. Israel he wanted to put such carriage-lamps on it, but the brethren holds that them's too stylish. So I sayed he ain't to put none on. I wouldn't want to set my childern a bad example to be wain that way."

"But carriage-lamps are useful," Acker suggested.

"You won't never see 'em on no Amish carriage," Levi answered. "We don't uphold to carriage-lamps."

They had reached Israel Baer's carriage shop at the end of the village street.

"I'll just take the new carriage with," he told the proprietor, "if you and your man kin hitch it behind this here wagon."

In a few minutes the new carriage, a well-made surrey polished like a piano, was drawn out to the street. Levi got out to inspect it carefully, while Sabina and Augustus looked on with interest.

"Well, does it suit?" Israel asked, as he regarded his handiwork with pride; while his trimmer stood ready to hitch it behind the other wagon.

"Yes, it suits all right," Levi nodded.

He drew out his purse and counted out one hundred and forty dollars. "There's your price. I'm satisfied if yous are."

"T'ank you, Levi. It ain't everyone pays cash as soon as a job's done a'ready. But that's the way with yous Amish—yous don't buy nothin' till yous have the money to pay for it; ain't?"

"We practise to be honest," Levi gravely returned. "Will you please fetch me a bucket of muddy water and a broom out?"

The trimmer stared at him. "A bucket of muddy water yet! What fur?"

"Well, you just fetch it here onct. And a broom."

In a few minutes the bucket of dirty water stood at Levi's feet and the broom was in his hand. Acker and Sabina both leaned out, curious to see what he was going to do.

Dipping the broom deep into the bucket, he deliberately rubbed it all over the beautiful, polished surface of his new carriage, to the utter ruin of its fine appearance.

Israel started forward and grasped his arm. "What you do, Levi!" he gasped. "Nothin' but a soft sponge and chamois had ought to touch that fine polish. Are you crazy or what?"

"It's too proud," returned Levi, calmly. "I couldn't take it on behind, lookin' that proud. I got to make it look humbler."

Again he dipped the broom into the bucket and scratched its rough corn over his carriage.

The trimmer, a stalwart man of middle age, looked suddenly apoplectic. "Damn you!" he cried. "You damned old fool, spoilin' the appearance of our good job like that there! What d'you pay your good money down fur if you want a dirty-lookin' scratched-up thing!"

Levi went on with his work of spoiling his carriage.

"You old long-haired hooks-and-eyes!" cried the trimmer, furiously, "I'd like to kick you good!"

"Here, now, come, come," Israel warned him, though he looked nearly as angry as his employee. "We got our money. It matters us nussing if he wants to be so bigoty!"

The trimmer turned his back upon Levi in infinite disgust and strode into the shop.

"Much obliged fur the loan of your bucket and broom," said Levi, gently. "I'm well suited with the carriage now."

He climbed up beside Acker, took the reins from his hand, and, with a nod to Israel, started down the road toward home.

Acker, at first, was incensed at such pious vandalism; but presently his sense of the ludicrous asserted itself, and he wondered how Levi's daughter felt about it. He glanced at her once or twice, but her face, like her father's, was non-committal.

They rode in solemn silence until they came to two diverging roads at the edge of the village. The horse, evidently from force of habit, turned to the right. But suddenly Sabina started forward from her seat at the back, and grasped her father's arm with one hand and the reins with the other, her face white, her eyes dilated.

"Take the road to the left!" she gasped.

Levi stopped the horse and turned to look at her, in vague alarm. Acker glanced up the road

to the right to see what had frightened her.
There was nothing to be seen except a smart-
looking phaeton that had entered the road just
ahead of them.

"What fur, Biney?" her father asked gently.

"You mustn't go down this here lane," she
faltered. "I—see the Face—down there!"

Acker felt an unaccountable chill as he heard
her, even while he was conscious of the pene-
trating sweetness of her voice.

"It can't nothin' happen us goin' straight
home," Levi argued. "It's too far by the other
road. Ain't, Biney?" he said coaxingly.

"We must not go home this a-way, pop!" she
said very solemnly.

"This is a foolishness, Biney!"

"Indeed, no, pop!"

He hesitated an instant, then yielded and
backed the horse to turn him to the left, while
Acker sat silent and bewildered.

Sabina sank back again in her seat, and
Levi's face was grave and troubled; and Acker
somehow felt that it would be unwelcome
impertinence to ask the wondering questions
which sprang to his lips. Presently he broke the
silence with a perfunctory remark.

"It's a pleasant day for a drive—not too hot,"
he said, turning to Sabina.

"It gives such changey weather," she murmured shyly.

"The paper wants rain," Levi inserted.

"Are you a member of the Amish church—or meeting, I believe you say?" Acker asked Sabina.

"Not yet," she replied. "Me and Aaron, us we'll mebbe join till fall."

"You differ from the Mennonites in wearing the garb before joining the church?" he inquired.

"Yes, we wear ourselves plain since we're born a'ready," she answered, venturing to raise her eyes to his face for an instant, and again he was simultaneously thrilled and chilled by their expression. It seemed to him that it must be the outward sign of some strange and even abnormal quality of mind.

"There's Noah Baker's place," Levi interrupted. "He's our neighbor. We're only half a mile from home now."

As they came nearer they saw Noah Baker standing at his gate, and at sight of them he came out into the road and motioned to Levi to stop.

"Why d'you come home this a-way, Levi?" he inquired with the frank curiosity as to one another's affairs that obtains among these rural people.

"Och," Levi spoke in evident embarrassment, "Biney she's along and she sayed she'd like to come this a-way."

"Fur a longer ride, ain't? Well, it was mebbe the hand of Providence kep' you from takin' the other road home!" cried Noah. "They're havin' a wonderful time over there in the right road! A city horse and buggy come along a quarter'n hour back, and got scairt at a road engine, and throwed over the buggy, and run into Ezra Herr's buggy where was tryin' to git past 'em in the narrer part, and och, it's a wonderful tangle they're in! Pete Zook come along and tole me. He says Ezra he's got his leg broke yet! And the city feller's brain's concussed or what; and they're sendin' him to the Lancaster hospital in. Och my, it done somepin' awful over there! To think, now, you choosed this left road! Else yous all might of been kilt yet!"

"Yes, ain't!" Levi said huskily, wiping the sweat from his brow.

Acker, marveling, glanced back at Sabina. But her head was bent low, and he could not see her face.

Without another look toward Noah, Levi gathered up his reins and started down the road.

Not a word was spoken by any of them until, some moments later, they reached the Wilt farm.

All the members of the Wilt household (excepting the nine-weeks-old baby and Aunt Susanna, who was dishing up the supper in the kitchen) were assembled on the front porch to witness the double event of the arrival of the new carriage and the city boarder. Acker found himself under a battery of frankly curious eyes as he got out of the wagon, and he felt rather glad that there was the new carriage to divide attention.

Now it chanced that Ulmer Popple, on his way home from the village, had stopped a second time at the Wilt farm to see Sabina, getting there about the time that Levi drove up to the house. Ulmer had hitched his horse near the barn and had come around to the front of the house just in time to see the stranger gallantly assisting Sabina out of the wagon, and his heart grew hot within him.

As her father led the stranger up to the porch to meet the family, Sabina found herself face to face with her scowling lover.

"Who's that there man anyhow?" he demanded, standing in front of her and thrusting his face close to her own.

"Ulmer," she protested in an injured voice, "you have no need to speak that close!"

Ulmer saw how white she looked, and he interpreted it as a sign of her guilty conscience.

"I want to know who that there dude is a-drivin' with you and a-liftin' his hat off to you! A-liftin' his hat to an *Amish* girl yet! And after you wouldn't go with me, too!"

"Well, if you must know, Ulmer, he's our boarder where's goin' to stay here a month. He ast pop at market to take him to board."

"He's goin' to live here a month!" Ulmer exclaimed.

"Yes."

"And you wouldn't go with me this after because you wanted to go with your pop to meet *him!*"

"If that's what you want to think, Ulmer Popple, you can think it!"

"What's that feller wantin' to board out here fur?" he demanded.

"I don't know right what fur. He's such a artist where draws pictures."

"Oh!" said Ulmer, mockingly, "he's an *educated* person, is he? Well, *educated* persons are mebbe all right when they're *honest!* But if that feller ain't a sharper, he deceives his appearance, that's all!"

"I'll let you and Aunt Susanna to worry about that," retorted Sabina.

"Oh, you will, will you? Well, what'll you do, Biney Wilt, when I leave off comin' over here to set up and keep comp'ny with you?" he threatened.

"What I'll do? What I done some more times—wait till you get over it!"

"Look a-here! D'you know what I'll do? You keep on a-makin' up with this here dude and I'll up and keep comp'ny with Elephena. How will you and your brother Aaron like *that*, huh?"

"You must be hard up, Ulmer, to be takin' another feller's girl. Elephena she liked Aaron this long time a'ready, and she wouldn't do it to go with another one."

"Well," said Ulmer, with the confidence of a wide experience of the sex and of his attractions for them, "you'll see onct! I'm better fixed than Aaron. . . . You promise me, Biney, you won't speak to that there feller in there again, and I'll leave Elephena be."

"It wouldn't be very genteel—such behavior—not speakin' to a party boardin' with us," Biney pleaded.

"All right! You look out!" and Ulmer turned and walked off.

She stood where he left her, her eyes anxiously following him as he went to the barn and unhitched his horse. Should she call him hack and promise—for Aaron's sake? He drew in his horse to a walk as he reached the front gate and glanced back at her; and she felt a pang of pity at sight of his miserable, sullen face.

But she remained silent and watched him out of sight.

Just as Mrs. Wilt was hospitably offering to escort her boarder to the kitchen pump that he might wash his face and hands before supper, Aaron caught sight of Elephena hurrying up the road toward him.

He turned about in surprise and went to meet her. It was seldom, indeed, that Elephena could escape her mother's watchful eye and come to visit her lover's "folks."

"Och, Aaron!" she cried excitedly, as he joined her just outside the gate, "what you think? Mom went off on comp'ny to New Holland over, and so I just snuk over here to see—to see—well, to see Biney onct!"

She cocked her pretty flaxen head and looked at him saucily.

"Are you sure it's to see Biney you come?" he gravely asked her.

"Why, to be sure! Who else, Aaron?"

"Ain't you heard about our city boarder?"

"What? Your city boarder? Oh, Aaron! Do you mean you got a young lady from the city stoppin' here?"

The jealous apprehension in her voice made Aaron, in his relief, laugh aloud, as an Amishman, whose bearing is for the most part of an oppressive gravity and sedateness, seldom does.

"It ain't no lady," he assured her. "It's a male. He come from Lancaster out."

"Oh!" breathed Elephena. "Will I see him if I stay and eat along?"

"Have you dare to stay?"

"Well, Aaron Wilt! I don't call that wery *hospitable*! I tole you I snuk off because she went off on comp'ny. She is stayin' fur the rest part of the night and won't be back till tomorrow."

Elephena's mother, who was a widow, kept the inn at the nearby village of Elim, and Elephena was her only child.

"I'm such afraid, Aaron," Elephena continued, clinging to his hand, "if mom finds out I come here today! This is Saturday, you know, and as a general our hired girl has off Saturday nights to go to New Holland in. But I plagued her to stay home and leave me go just this onct.

But supposin' she'd forget herself and leave out
to mom that I come here!"

Elephena turned pale at the bare thought.
"It was only yesterday I heard mom talkin' to
an agent that come fur dinner, how she hated
them broad-brimmed-hat fellers that lived
around here! Oh, Aaron, she talks down on
yous Amish wonderful strong!"

"That needn't make you any difference, Elephena," Aaron comforted her. "*She* don't have
to like us and our broad-brimmed hats. I ain't
astin' *her* to marry me."

"Oh, Aaron, you don't know her. She'll never
give in. Mom was always so much fur just *rulin'*
me, whether it was fur any reason or not, and
I always knowed when it come to my marryin'
she'd want to pick out my gent'man friend—
or else she'd go ag'in' him. And then when
I choosed an Amishman yet! Well, she took
on—it was something terrible!" Elephena half
gasped at the recollection. "You see," she continued plaintively, as together they sat down
on the porch steps, Aaron still keeping her
hand in his, "mom got me raised to be such
afraid of her, I don't know how to go ag'in'
her. You ain't got no idea, Aaron, how hard
mom used to be to me when I was only a little
girl yet. Yous Amish is always so gentle to each

other in your families, it would sound queer to you if I tole you how mom used to treat me. An' she ain't no different to what she was. I darsent cross her none. So long as I do just what she wants and ast her dare I do every-thing, then she's wonderful good to me; but if I take my own head fur one thing—even to what fur frock I shall put on yet! Then she's that ugly to me!"

"Never mind, Elephena!" Aaron said ten-derly. "Just as soon as you can make up your mind to join meetin' and wear yourself plain you can come right over to our place and stay, and we'll get married right aways and live here till we're got a house ready where pop says he'll give us. I don't know what makes you hesitate so long, Elephena," he urged.

"But, Aaron," she demanded plaintively, "it ain't any more fur you to turn Lutheran than fur me to turn plain. I can't see, if you want me so bad, why you won't turn Lutheran to get me."

"I can't join with the world's people, Ele-phena," he answered, going over the arguments he was wont to advance whenever the subject was broached. "And yours is a fash'nable church of the world. Us Amish knows better'n to take up with them wain and carnal doctrines.

I'd be cuttin' myself off from all my own people, too, and from all the ways I was brought up to."

"Well, and so would I if I joined on to the Amish."

"It's for the man to be the head of the woman, Scripture says, Elephena. So you ought to yield up to me."

"And if I won't do it, Aaron?"

"But you will, Elephena," he returned, an obstinate conviction mingled with the fondness in his tone.

"But if I *don't?*" she persisted.

"But you're a-goin' to, someday."

"Well, but if I don't would you give me up before you'd give up your Amish convictions?"

"But I ain't havin' to give you up. You'll turn plain."

"But if I *don't,* then?" she cried, a touch of temper in her voice. "If I don't, *don't,* DON'T?"

"I know you will if I just wait long enough," Aaron's sweet voice replied.

"Aaron Wilt, if you ain't stubborn-headed!" She gave up in despair. "If this here's how stubborn you're goin' to be after we're married!"

"I'll never use you mean," he tenderly assured her. "To be sure, a man's the head of the wife, fur the Bible says so."

Aunt Susanna's voice calling Aaron to supper interrupted them.

"They'll be that surprised to see you, Elephena!" Aaron smiled as they rose from the porch steps and went into the kitchen.

CHAPTER THREE

Aunt Susanna Catechizes

It was nearly two hours after the early supper at the Wilt farm, and all the evening chores were finished; the cows were milked, the milk "separated," the dishes washed, and the baby put to bed; and now the family went out on the front porch to join the boarder, who had been sitting there alone in the soft summer evening.

The Wilt family was not in the habit of squandering time in sitting on the front porch even at night; and it had been Sabina's awkward solicitation that led them thus to set aside their usual custom of going to bed as soon as the work was done. "Leave us come out and set a while with *him*," she had coaxed her mother; "it ain't sociable not to. Mebbe he has homesick."

Mrs. Wilt yielded, and of course her husband went with her; Aunt Susanna, Aaron, Elephena, and small Samuel and Melinda all followed.

Acker rose to assist Sabina in dragging out two heavy rocking chairs from the front room. Not accustomed to such politeness, the girl grew crimson with mingled pleasure and embarrassment. When Acker insisted that she sit in the rocking chair and let him take the porch step at her feet—which, seeing he was "comp'ny," was a shameful reversal of the proper order of things—her pretty confusion quite charmed him.

"We can't set long," Mrs. Wilt said, as she gently rocked in her huge chair, "or else we couldn't get up early enough in the morning."

"What time must I be ready for breakfast?" Acker inquired.

"Och, you needn't eat along with us at breakfast. We eat too early—at four o'clock a'ready. When you feel fur comin' down, me or my sister, the hired girl"—indicating Aunt Susanna—"will make you some fried eggs or what."

"Thank you," said Acker. "I would think it nothing short of criminal to get up at four o'clock. How do you manage to do it?"

"Well, we mostly go to bed right after the evening work's through a'ready."

"Tomorrow is Sunday; do you have to get up so early on Sunday?"

"Yes, there's the milking and all the chores to do; and tomorrow we have meetin' over to

Adam Finefrock's. You know us Amish don't have meetin'-houses. We just meet at the homes of the brethren. We'll have to get up early to get over there in time."

"Do you never take any time for pleasure?" he inquired.

"Yes," Levi answered his question. "We go, still, on weddin's and funerals. And onct me and Naomi and Susanna we went to Phil'delphy."

Suddenly Aunt Susanna shot a question at him with the abruptness of a pop-gun and in her characteristic tone of dark suspicion.

"Where's your folks, anyhow?"

"My folks?"

"Yes, your folks. Ain't you got no folks?"

"Oh, yes. They are in different places just at present."

Acker observed that the family listened sharply to hear him give an account of himself. Sabina, especially, seemed to await his answers with bated breath.

"In different places?" Aunt Susanna repeated curiously. "What fur is that? Why ain't they together? And why," she asked, her sense of politeness evidently warring with her doubts of him, "ain't you along?"

"I suppose because I am here," Acker answered, with such a pleasant smile that, while baffled, Aunt Susanna could not possibly feel affronted.

But she continued: "Does your folks know where you're at?"

"Some of them do."

"Where is your home, anyhow?" asked Levi.

"In Baltimore."

"Is your parents livin'?" asked Naomi.

"My father, yes."

"Have you any children?" demanded Aunt Susanna.

"I'm not married."

"Och!" she said in confusion. "That's the time I spoke too soon, ain't? Then your mom's passed away?"

"Yes."

"Did she die long a'ready?"

"Ten years ago."

"Have you any sisters or brothers?"

"One brother."

"Does he work anything?"

"He's trying to work the government just now for a job. I hope he gets it."

"What does your pop work?" Mrs. Wilt asked.

"He is a minister."

"One of these here paid, world-made ministers?" Aunt Susanna's disapproving tones demanded.

"I am bound to acknowledge it."

"Now," said Aaron, looking up from Elephena's face to regard the boarder with his soft, cow-like eyes, "what does your pop make a year at that?"

"What most other ministers of the Episcopal Church make—enough to stave off starvation," answered Acker.

He began to feel a little restive under this catechism, but he was curious to see how far they would go.

"Did your pop have to go to one of these here cemeteries of theology to get made a preacher?" Levi asked.

"A theological seminary? Oh, yes."

"Them cemeteries can't make preachers out of a man," the other affirmed dogmatically. "It's the Lord's got to do that. Now us, we don't make our preachers at no preacher-mill! Ourn is homemade preachers, choosed right out of our congregation by a wote of the members."

"Yes?" said Acker, respectfully.

"I'd think," said Aunt Susanna, "your folks would feel some oneasy havin' you away. You're so poor-lookin'."

Acker regarded this doubtful compliment with uncertainty.

"You're so thin at yourself. You ain't got much spec [fat] on your bones, and you're so pale that way. I wouldn't doubt that mebbe you was consumpted. My man he was just so poor-lookin', and he died off for me."

Acker began to feel that it was no wonder Aunt Susanna's "man" had "died off"; probably he had done it from choice.

The sound of carriage wheels falling upon the evening stillness, just now, caused a sensation in the little group on the porch. The curiosity to see whose carriage it was lent an animation to the placid faces of the Wilts that one would not have deemed possible. Samuel and Melinda ran to the fence to have a look at the passerby.

It struck Acker as a significant fact that a family who could be so interested in the passing of a chance vehicle and in the personal affairs of a stranger like himself should not discuss or even refer to such a serious accident to one of their neighbors as that which had occurred that afternoon in "the right road." One would have expected it to be an all-absorbing topic this evening.

"It's John Hinerdeer and his wife," announced Aunt Susanna. "But I couldn't see who the other party was with 'em."

"Elephena! It was your mom along with 'em!" cried Sabina, in a soft voice of alarm. "*Now* what's to do?"

Her timid glance rested for an instant on
the figure sitting at her feet, in his "world's
garb," so sinfully alluring to her eye; the
smooth whiteness of his hands indicating, to
her at least, a life of elegant leisure; his face
bearing none of the marks of commonplace
toil under the hot sun, but pale and fine, and
so wholly unlike any other she had ever seen;
and Sabina knew, with secret pain at her own
perfidy, that whatever might befall her
brother, from Ulmer's threat that he would
go and court Elephena, she did not, in her
heart, regret that she had not bound herself
by a promise to abstain from speaking to this
fascinating man.

"Oh," gasped Elephena, "that didn't look
near like my mom! Did *you* think, Aaron, it
was mom?"

"It looked a little like her shape," Aaron
reluctantly admitted.

"Tell me," Elephena nervously insisted, "do
you *know* if it was mom? Don't keep it back from
me, Aaron!"

"Yes," said Aaron, gently. "I'm near sure
it was."

"She sayed she wouldn't get home till tomorrow morning!" Elephena lamented. "If only
I'd started home sooner and got there first!

Well," she sighed, "I got to go right aways back now, anyhow."

The girl said good night to the family, adding a shy adieu to the stranger, and then she and Aaron started away in the summer twilight.

"How far has she to go?" Acker asked.

"Two mile," Levi answered. "To Elim. It's a hotel over, and her mom keeps it."

"Mebbe her mom won't make awful, when she finds Elephena snuk over here!" said Aunt Susanna. "Yes, yes," she sighed, "as the sayin' goes, 'Happy who is single yet, sad who is engaged.'"

"It's time we was all went to bed," said Mr. Wilt, rising and taking Samuel and Melinda in hand to lead them into the house. "It's near eight o'clock. We ain't used to settin' up this late," he explained to Acker. "I guess you city people's used to set up till as late, mebbe, as *nine* o'clock yet—ain't?"

"Some have been known to do it," granted Acker, gravely, as he hastened to prevent Aunt Susanna from carrying in the heavy rocking chairs. Levi made no movement to help her, for an Amishman's idea of the relation of the sexes is not unlike that of a North American Indian— it is the part of the female to wait on the male and make him comfortable. This, indeed, is the chief end of woman.

"I 'most forgot to ast you," said Mrs. Wilt, "what you'd mebbe like fur your breakfast. As a general, all we have fur breakfast is eggs and dried beef and coffee, jelly, bread, and pie and cake. That mebbe wouldn't be enough fur you. Are you some sneaky about your wittles?"

In his uncertainty as to what the question meant, Acker, after an instant's hesitation, answered at a venture, "I trust I'm not *that!*"

He was going to announce that he would stay downstairs in the cool sitting room and read for a few hours; but he felt that Aunt Susanna would regard such a proposal with suspicion. So he meekly followed Sabina upstairs, resigning himself to the necessity of reading by the dim light of a small kerosene lamp in a hot bedroom under the roof.

As he said good night to Sabina at the door of his room, he was struck afresh by the expression of her eyes—they seemed to narrow and elongate as they met his, as though the girl saw beyond what was manifest to ordinary vision. Her conscious blush betrayed with unsophisticated candor the magnetism she felt in his masculine presence.

Acker stood in the middle of his room and looked about him. It was a large, square apartment under a sloping roof. There was no carpet on the rough, unpainted floor. The room contained two old-fashioned beds, a long wooden chest, a high ponderous bureau, and several wooden chairs decorated with luridly painted flowers. Spread out on top of the chest and the bureau was a remarkable medley of five-cent glass and china dishes and ornaments. Suspended from hooks on the four walls were gowns of bright purple, green, and blue, several suits of men's clothing, and several broad-brimmed black felt Amish hats. The pillowcases on both beds were elaborately embroidered in red cotton; the embroidery on one of them represented a cherub labeled "Fast Asleep," on the other "Wide Awake." The red cotton features of these cherubs were rather gruesome and inhuman. A crescent and four stars kept guard over the Fast Asleep cherub, and butterflies hovered over the head of the Wide Awake one. On the edge of each pillowcase was embroidered, "Levi Wilt and Naomi Wilt. 1885." A small decorated card, bearing a printed name, peeped out of each piece of china and glass. Acker surmised that these cards bore the names of the donors of the tawdry gifts—evidently wedding gifts to Levi and Naomi. Economy and thrift being the ruling motives of even the wealthiest among the Amish, who, as a class, are very prosperous, a five- or ten-cent piece of glass or china was looked upon as a sufficiently generous bridal offering.

Acker curiously handled some of the clothes hanging about the room. The material of the gowns was as cheap as possible. That of the men's clothing was a trifle better. He smiled as he saw the hooks and eyes on coats, vests, and trousers.

He had already gathered from his talk with the family that many customs rigidly adhered to by the Amish are followed, not so much from conviction, as from mere tenacity of habit; for in the several generations that have passed away since the founding of the sect, the origin and meaning of some of their austere rules have been lost sight of. But, like the devotees of some more enlightened faiths, this fact in no wise weakens their strict observance of them.

The realization came to Acker with a sudden sense of consternation that there were no toilet appointments whatever in the room, no washstand, no towels, no mirror. He remembered having heard that mirrors, being considered a vanity, were prohibited by the Meeting. What should he do? By this time the household was all abed, and he could not summon anyone to rescue him from his absurd plight.

"Do they expect me to perform all my ablutions at the kitchen pump, as I was invited to do before supper?" he wondered.

Slate-colored coffee, eggs fried in lard, and "snitz-pie" one could grow accustomed to; but, to a man of his fastidious habits, not to be able to indulge in the luxury of a morning bath was a situation nothing short of tragic.

He retired slightly depressed in spirit, with the resolve that in the morning he would gently but firmly insist upon better toilet arrangements.

CHAPTER FOUR

An Amish Sabbath

AMONG HIS ACQUAINTANCES AND FRIENDS—
especially those of the other sex—Augustus
Acker was considered to be a young man of
attractive personality; and had he been at all
inclined to egotism, the influences to induce
this rather chronic malady of young artists were
not lacking. But while he was too observant not
to know that girls generally admired him, he
was, strangely enough, quite modest as to his
own attractions; and despite all the flattering
attention to which he was subjected, he was neither cynical nor self-conscious. He was, however,
very susceptible to feminine charm; so much so
that there were times when the star to which he
had hitched his wagon, when determining to
consecrate his life to Art, had threatened to dis-
appear. Here was Sabina, for instance, sitting at
his side on this balmy Sabbath morning, as they

slowly drove to meeting, as fresh and sweet a bit of young girlhood as his eyes had ever rested upon; and even though he must, perforce, look upon her much as he would look upon his father's cook—barring that unique quality which seemed to set her apart from her kind— he was tempted to throw prudence to the winds and make love to her recklessly.

Consideration for the girl, however, restrained him. Quite transitory and meaningless ardor on his part might signify too much to this unso-phisticated country damsel; and his sense of honor forbade that he should take advantage of the hospitality and confidence extended to him in this primitive household to work possible havoc in the heart of the daughter.

"How did Elephena fare last night at the hands of her irate mother?" inquired Acker.

"Aaron sayed Elephena's mom took on some-thing turrible," Sabina's mellow voice replied. "Elephena she wouldn't leave him go in the house with her—she sayed that would make her mom all the madder. So Aaron listened outside the kitchen, and he come on home awful downhearted."

"Do you think they'll ever marry?" Acker asked.

"If—if other ones keeps away and don't coax Elephena off from Aaron," she faltered. "But, anyways, unlest Elephena she joins Amish meetin', Aaron wouldn't marry her."

"And do you feel the same way? Wouldn't you marry anyone but an Amishman?"

Sabina blushed deeply, and her shy voice was unsteady as she answered: "Whether I'd marry anyone but an Amishman? I ain't never thought so far. I never kep' comp'ny with no one but Ulmer Popple. He's Amish. But," she hastily added, "we ain't promised. I can't make up my mind."

"You do not wear a ring?" he asked, glancing down at her left hand.

She looked up at him inquiringly. "What fur ring is that? Us Amish we don't favor jewels."

"You don't have engagement rings?"

Sabina shook her head. "Is that one of the world's customs?"

"Didn't you ever hear of it, Biney?" he asked wonderingly.

"What—'engagement rings?' Och, no. Tell me onct. I'd like to hear about 'em."

He explained the custom to her, and she listened enthralled.

"The ring is the symbol of unending love, you know."

Her face glowed as she heard him. "Some of the world's ways is pleasing, ain't?" she said wistfully. "I—I'd like such a ring when I was promised. But I know"—she sighed—"that them's wanities where is of the devil."

"Don't you be so sure of that, Biney," he began, but he checked himself. Why disturb her simple superstitions? To doubt the traditions of her people could only bring her unhappiness.

"Ulmer doesn't know how to manage you," he said, turning to her with a smile. "If I were in his place I'd bring you to terms by flirting with—Jemima."

"Jemima who?" Sabina asked wonderingly.

"Any Jemima that happened to be at hand when you were by."

"It ain't no girl named Jemima livin' near here."

"Well, then, Jane or Sarah, or anyone—I'd not be particular."

"What's 'flirting'?"

"What's flirting?" he repeated, considering. "Making love without meaning it."

"Not meaning it fur really?"

"That's the idea."

"Oh! Is it *that* where you mean? But Ulmer he did try that a'ready. But somehow I don't mind if he goes with other ones."

"Then you don't like him?"

"I never felt fur gettin' married to him," she granted.

"Poor Ulmer Popple!"

"There's plenty other ones would like to have him and can't get him. He's so set on havin' me."

"I believe your Aunt Susanna said he would be at meeting this morning."

"I guess," nodded Sabina.

"You must point him out to me. By the way, where is the meeting held—where are we going?"

"Over to Buckart's; it's at Adam Finefrock's we have meetin' today."

"At a private house?"

"Yes. Us Amish we don't uphold to havin' meetin'-houses. We take turns and meet onct in two weeks at the house of one of the members. There's so many of us round here, it takes a year and a half to get round to all the houses."

"Will one house hold all who want to come?"

"Well, it ain't always handy—sometimes we have to crowd pretty close. But us Amish we have our kitchens built wery big, and the other rooms all open into the kitchen. Adam Finefrock's got a big kitchen. His farm's right on the end of the willage street, next door to the Lutheran minister's. The Lutheran minister he's Elephena's mom's preacher. He come to Buckart's only a couple months back a'ready, from away somewheres, fetchin' a wife along from Phil'delphy, and och, my! But he's got a dumn wife! Just think, *she can't make lard!* . . . Well, to be sure, I always heard city women was wery poor wives. It's the country girls makes the good wives," concluded Sabina, with so much feeling that Acker's eyes curiously sought her face under its ugly purple bonnet.

"The preacher he has three churches," she continued; "and he makes a good bit; but it *takes* a good bit fur such a wife. . . . Would *you* marry a girl where couldn't make lard?"

"I'm afraid I wouldn't marry one that *could*," Acker answered grimly, thinking it wise she should realize that her point of view was not his.

Sabina looked bewildered at his answer and fell into a silent consideration of it.

Presently she remarked: "You'll have a lot to explain to your folks about our ways so different, when you go home, ain't?"

"I shouldn't wonder if I did."

"Like our schoolteacher explained to us about folks so different, too. Now the Japanese are different to us again."

"Yes."

"I never went off much. I don't know about traveling. Lancaster's all the further I traveled a'ready."

"Should you like to travel and see the world?"

"I often thought I'd like to see Phil'delphy onct."

Acker could not repress a smile at the simplicity which could call Philadelphia "the world."

"Here we're comin' to Buckart's," she announced as the neat village street came into view ahead of them. "And och, if there ain't Ulmer Popple in his buggy—with Elephena!"

Consternation and distress were in her voice.

"Is that Ulmer?" Acker asked, looking with interest at the stalwart youth in the approaching buggy.

"Yes. And Elephena with!"

"Elephena must be fickle."

"What's—what's that again?" Sabina timidly asked.

"Fickle? I mean why doesn't she stick to Aaron?"

"I guess her mom made her go with Ulmer when he ast her, just to spite Aaron."

"But Ulmer's an Amishman. I thought Mrs. Schwenkfelders' objection to Aaron was that he was an Amishman."

"She's down on all us Wilts. And Ulmer's so much better fixed than Aaron, she'd mebbe overlook it that he's Amish. And mebbe she thinks she could get Ulmer to join on to the world's ways. She knows Aaron wouldn't near do that."

"Will Aaron see Elephena here with Ulmer?"

"To be sure. And how he'll feel yet!"

Acker drew up in line behind the long row of Amish carriages that filled the road, while, at the same time, Ulmer went out of his way to bring up ostentatiously abreast of him.

"He doesn't know how to play his part," Acker thought as he saw the jealous looks the young man directed toward them, unmindful of Elephena at his side.

"Well, Biney," Elephena greeted Sabina uncertainly, as the two damsels were simultaneously assisted to the ground. "Well, 'Gustus," she nodded to Acker with more confidence.

Sabina acknowledged Elephena's greeting a little coolly, but spoke to Ulmer with ingratiating friendliness: "Well, Ulmer."

Ulmer gave her a look of mingled injury and rage, and did not answer as he proceeded to tie his horse.

Acker's was the sixty-fifth of the white canvas-covered wagons that surrounded Adam Finefrock's place, all of them so exactly alike that the casual observer would have been greatly puzzled to know how each distinguished his own property.

"I'd better mark this wagon, for I'll never know it from all the rest," Acker said to Sabina, as she stood at his side while he tied the horse.

"I'll know it," Sabina assured him.

"But how?"

"Oh, we just look at 'em and then we know ourn. I wonder if Elephena she thinks Ulmer Popple he means it fur *really* when he takes her buggy-ridin' to meetin'," Sabina speculated anxiously as she and Acker walked up the board walk toward the yellow-painted house. "All the Amish girls wants him. He's so well fixed."

"How do you happen to be an exception?"

"D'you mean why I don't want him? Well, sometimes I think I'm *contrary* that way. Ulmer he can't believe I ain't like the other ones—just crazy to have him. But I can't help tryin' to learn him that *I* don't think he's only got to say 'snip' for me to say 'snap.'"

Biney flushed to find herself talking so much and so freely. Her new acquaintance moved her to confidences and to an expression of herself that was unusual.

Acker was half amused at himself as he realized what a sympathetic and lively interest he felt in all aspects of this primitive rural drama that was being enacted under his eyes.

The kitchen which they entered was, to use Sabina's words, "settin' full of people"; and they were obliged to sit in the parlor, which was not so entirely filled. This parlor was furnished almost exactly like the one at the Wilt farm—"piece carpet" on the floor, china and glass dishes thickly covering every available flat surface, and clothes hanging from the whitewashed walls.

Acker was conscious that he was the object of much curiosity. As the meeting was not yet opened, the people were chatting together sociably in the vernacular of the Pennsylvania German. Very little of this was intelligible to Acker, in spite of his knowledge of German.

The service was presently opened by the singing of a hymn in the same hybrid tongue. Of course there was no organ accompaniment, musical instruments being considered an invention of the devil. A more dreary attempt at harmony Acker had never heard than the monotonous droning of this Amish hymn.

What perhaps interested him more than any other feature were the children, from two to six years old, who were ranged along the wall in the room where he sat. They were as demure and solemn as their elders. The big lusty Amishmen in their odd garb sat in thoughtful attitudes, following with earnest attention every word of the service.

Acker observed that every Amishman as he entered the house threw his wide-brimmed hat upon a window seat, till there were several big piles of them. These hats were all so exactly alike in size, color, and shape that he found himself speculating profoundly on the inscrutable problem as to how in the name of all the gods each was to pick out his own headgear. It was apparently a worse problem than that of the wagons.

The rest of the service proceeded in the "Dutch" dialect, and a panic seized Acker at the thought of having to sit through an hour of this hot summer's morning under the preaching of an unintelligible sermon. "Does the minister preach in Dutch?" he whispered to Sabina.

She nodded.

"How long does he usually preach?"

"Not more than two hours, still."

"Och Gott!" muttered Acker. "That settles it. I'm going out for a walk! I'll be back for you, Sabina, later."

He rose hastily and picked up his hat.

"You must be back in time to eat, ain't?" Her wistful eyes were raised to his face with a look that lamented his going.

"To eat?"

"We always eat dinner after the preaching."

"Here?"

"Yes, we eat wherever the meetin' is, still."

"Very well; I shall come back in two hours."

He wondered, as he slipped out of the open door, how the mistress of the house would manage to feed the scores of people crowded into those rooms.

He walked down the village street, and found himself, presently, in front of the Lutheran church. Through the open windows he saw that the large Sunday school room was crowded to the very doors. The Lutherans from all over the township were accustomed to worship here.

The Sunday school was singing lustily. He strolled in and sat down by the door, near a large class of young girls seated in a semicircle around a sleek young man who looked for all the world like the lord of a harem. The young man was self-consciously dressed in his Sunday store-clothes and wore a very pious countenance.

One of the maidens ventured forth from the harem to bring Acker a songbook. He rose and bowed his thanks as he received it, and the maiden smiled on him encouragingly and informed him that it was "Paterotic Day."

This fact accounted for the song they were singing, he decided as he sat down and followed the words which the school was shouting:

On, Pennsylvania! We are marching on.
Sabbath-school coworkers, we are
    marching on.
From our first convention in the
    country's dawn,
Onward, Pennsylvania! We are marching on!

At the conclusion of this remarkable hymn the superintendent rose and gazed around blandly on his expectant flock.

"We will now sing another piece called 'Awake,'" he announced from the platform. "But I think," he added facetiously, with an evidently keen relish for his own humor, "hardly any are asleep!"

This sally was greeted by great laughter, and the superintendent looked pleased with himself.

"Awake" was followed by the superintendent's address, to which specimen of religious oratory Acker listened with a sort of wondering interest.

He spoke of the comforts of religion offered in "a cheerless, charit-less world." He waxed eloquent and used what Sabina would have called "high language," being evidently fond of big words. Speaking of those who had gone to make their fortunes at the Klondike, he said: "They have wonderfully enhanced their competency financially, it is true. *But,* my dear young people"—he raised his voice to a shout and his hand in solemn warning—"if you want to gather gold, don't go to the Klondike! If you want to gather gold, don't go to California! If you want to gather diamonds, don't go to Brazil! All the gold and diamonds you want are right here—in Buckart's—*in the gospel of Christ!*"

Falling presently into patriotism, he foretold that the millennium was coming to the United States, whose boundaries would, before long, include both North and South America. "This great land of ours will stand when Gabriel comes! Other nations are passing away, but our great nation will stay!"

Its permanency, however, depended upon its acceptance of the superintendent's idea of religion. "First the Israelites rejected God; then the Jews rejected Christ; and now the world is losing its last chance by rejecting the Holy Ghost! Unless it repents and accepts the Holy Ghost, even this great nation of ours cannot stand!"

At this point Acker decided that a walk in the country would induce a more worshipful frame of mind; so he quietly slipped out.

Later, when he returned to Adam Finefrock's, the multitude had gathered about long tables, improvised for the occasion, in the kitchen, and was partaking of dinner. Many of the women present helped in the work of serving.

Sabina invited him to sit down with her, and no sooner were they seated than Ulmer quickly led Elephena to the places opposite.

Elephena, who, had she been born into another environment, would undoubtedly have been a coquette, appeared half pleased with Ulmer's ostentatious attentions and half mortified and troubled that Aaron's sister should be a witness to them. Aaron himself was not in evidence.

"Aaron he went straight home again," Sabina whispered in a choked voice to Acker.

In order that there should be no house-wifely rivalry, the church-dinner menu, Sabina told Acker, was invariably the same at every house: pickled beets, dried-apple pies (even in the apple season), coffee, molasses, apple-butter, and bread and butter. No plates or forks were used, but everyone was furnished with a knife which served him for several uses—to put "spreadin's" on his bread, to dip into the molasses or apple-butter, and to cut the pie.

Acker wondered, when he saw coffee being served, how any one house happened to have cups and saucers enough for so many guests; but that problem had been solved by using the same cups and saucers, without washing or rinsing, for each relay of guests, no one apparently objecting to the accumulating deposit of grounds in the bottom of his cup. Acker suddenly found that, in spite of his long walk, he was not hungry. And he found it hard to ignore the black looks which Ulmer directed toward him.

After dinner, before starting for home, Sabina attempted to have a word with Ulmer, but he snubbed her grandly.

"Choose your comp'ny with city fellers if you want!" he said scornfully. "*I* ain't hinderin' you. I'm suited good enough with Elephena Schwenkfelders!"

"If you'd suit yourself with a girl that wasn't another one's girl," Sabina retorted, "I wouldn't care. Why have you need to go and take Aaron's girl off of him?"

Ulmer flushed with anger at her unhappily thoughtless words. "She's suited with me better'n she's suited with Aaron," he said.

"Oh, Ulmer," Sabina expostulated, "you're that conceity about yourself! If you didn't always think yourself so much, still, mebbe you'd of got me to say yes before this."

"I don't want you to say yes. I'm better suited with Elephena."

"She ain't Amish."

"She'll turn fur *me*."

"Wery well, Ulmer," said Sabina.

She turned away, but Ulmer quickly checked her. "If you'll pass me your promise you won't run with that dude no more—"

Sabina wavered. Ulmer took instant offense at her hesitation.

"If he's your style, Biney, to be sure *my* style wouldn't suit you!"

Before she could stop him, he had turned to Elephena and was taking her out to his buggy.

CHAPTER FIVE

The Mystery of Sabina

ACKER HAD LITTLE OPPORTUNITY FOR SOLVING the mystery OF Sabina, for the girl was busy from morning to night.

He longed to sketch her beautiful, strange face; he felt that if he could do it justice it would bring him no little fame. But he saw that it would be impossible to get her permission; for not only would she never be able to take time from her almost slavish farm-work, but, as her religion forbade even the vanity of photographs, he could not hope that her conscience would sanction his painting her portrait. He considered whether he might tempt the Amish love of earning money and offer to pay her for posing for him. But he realized that, with an Amishman, not even his keenness for small profits could weigh against his jealous guarding of his conscientious scruples, especially as to all things counted "worldly." If he painted Sabina at all, it must be from memory. He determined to imprint her image so indelibly on his mind that he would not need the living model before him in order to transfer it to his canvas. And surreptitiously he made several memorandum pencil sketches.

Whenever he was in the girl's presence he received a vague impression from her general demeanor, no matter how busily at work she was, that she felt intensely conscious of him in a way that he could not quite understand, for her bearing did not suggest the sentimentality of the romantic girl as he knew the species.

He received an impression, also, of trouble in the air between her and Aaron, and the anxiety and even distress which he frequently saw in her countenance made him conscious of the struggle which was going on in her heart between her disinclination for her lover, Ulmer Popple, and her unwillingness to cause her brother pain.

"Biney, is Ulmer still offended with you for going to church with me?" he asked her one day when she had joined him for a moment on the porch.

Sabina nodded shamefacedly.

"Can't you make it up with him?"

"He's runnin' with Elephena now. He's at her place all his spare time."

"But he does that just to make you jealous. It's you, not Elephena, he cares for, isn't it?"

"I guess," she nodded.

"Then why don't you make it all right with him?"

Sabina drew a deep sigh. "If a body could!" she said.

"Is he so hard to propitiate—to satisfy?"

Suddenly she looked up at him, her eyes burning. "He wants me to pass my word I won't speak to you."

"But that's unreasonable. It would be so very inconvenient, seeing we are under one roof. He can't really want to hold you to any such absurd promise."

Sabina looked away again, and did not answer.

"I'm sure," he urged, "you can satisfy him with something less than that."

"I guess I could, mebbe. But," she said in a low voice, "I don't feel fur keepin' comp'ny with Ulmer."

"That's a pity, isn't it? For Aaron's sake, I mean."

Sabina stirred uneasily. "I did try to make up last Sunday, and Ulmer he wouldn't do it."

"Try again."

Sabina set her lips primly. "It ain't fur *me* to do the courtin'."

"Of course not," Acker heartily agreed. "And Ulmer doesn't deserve that you should be kind to him after his behavior. But for Aaron's sake—and Elephena's?"

"I'm wonderful sorry fur Aaron—but—but I'd be sorry fur myself, too, if I done what goes ag'in' me so!"

Acker felt a sudden respect for this simplicity of mind which could not act with disloyalty to its primitive instincts.

But before many more days had passed, it began to dawn upon him that Ulmer was not wholly unjustified in his jealousy, and that he himself was, without doubt, an object of romantic, if not tender, interest to the Amish damsel.

He realized that he must not encourage the girl in her evident fancy, both for her sake and for his own; for her beauty was very alluring.

Yet whenever she was near him, for the sake of that picture which he hoped would one day score him his best success, his eyes dwelt upon her in the effort to fix in his memory every line of her face and form.

Even his strolls about the country by day and evening, and his absorption of local color, all bore a vital relation to his study of Sabina, for he saw everything as a possible setting for his portrait of her.

One evening, just as he started out for a walk in the patch of beautiful woodland a short distance up the road, he encountered Sabina on the porch, and she looked at him with an appeal in her lovely eyes that he found hard to resist.

He hesitated an instant. The temptation to yield to her unspoken entreaty and invite her to go with him was very strong; not alone for her sake, either, he realized. But he merely nodded casually as he walked away.

Strolling about under the beautiful old trees of the forest, in the summer evening stillness, the image of those appealing eyes and all that they had spoken was vividly with him. His fancy strayed into pleasant channels, colored ever by the seriousness that was at the foundation of his character. Life was rich to him just now in his youth and strength—full to overflowing with passionate desires of which he felt the approaching realization, crowded with high purposes which his blood tingled to accomplish. As he felt the soft green earth under his feet and heard the gentle rustling of the leaves overhead and the evening music of insects and birds, the mere fact that he was alive thrilled him with joy.

But, looking, from the outside, upon the primitive and even sordid lives of these Amish people, he asked himself *was* life worth while to those to whom the universe in all its higher meaning was forever sealed? Of course, to these people themselves, their lives were of as great value as was his to him. Were we, then, all alike deluded, and was it only a relative matter, after all, as to who was the greatest dupe? His buoyant optimism repudiated the doubt.

"It is the misanthropes, the cynics, who are deluded. Not the man who finds joy in being alive, even though his joy is just a few degrees higher than the contentment of his cows," he said to himself.

His thoughts were suddenly arrested by the sound of footsteps. He was surprised, for in his many rambles in these woods he had never before met a living soul. In a few minutes he saw, strolling leisurely toward him in the path, Sabina herself, her eyes dreamily downcast, as though unconscious of his nearness.

He knew that she had come out to meet him and that her abstraction was merely pretense. It was an unprecedented thing that an Amish girl should waste time in an aimless walk alone in the woods, and Acker felt vaguely troubled.

She stopped within a few feet of him and turned to examine a wild flower. Acker was amused at the childish subterfuge. Even when he stopped at her side she did not look up, but continued absurdly to bend her attention upon the ground, as though unaware of his presence.

"Have you lost something?" he inquired seriously.

She lifted her head with a well-assumed start of surprise. "Oh, is it you, 'Gustus? I'm just on my way back from astin' Sallie Shenk fur her pattern fur such a bureau-cover she promised me this long time a'ready," she said, deliberately turning to walk on at his side, though shame at her own boldness made her blush deeply. "So this evening," she added as they walked on together, "I thought I might as well go get it onct. Then I conceited I'd come home this a-way, through the woods."

"Yes?"

"I think, *too,* it's some pretty walkin' in the woods. It wouldn't be easy fur me to find the time, often, because we have eight cows and I must milk all. The young lady schoolteacher we had last spring she was so much fur comin' out here in these woods. She liked it too. I come with her onct or twict."

Acker had taken off his hat and was fanning his face with it as they walked.

"It's some warm tonight, too; say it is?" Biney remarked.

"It is," he rejoined laconically.

They had come to the edge of the woods and had wandered into a neighboring graveyard back of an old German Reformed church. As they passed among the stones, Sabina repeated the names of the dead, with an air of conveying interesting information.

"Here Mary Schlegemilch lays," she announced solemnly.

"Who was Mary Schlegemilch?" he inquired, supposing the fact to have some significance.

"She was the daughter of Mr. and Mrs. Schlegemilch."

"Oh!" murmured Acker. He bent to read the tombstone inscription in the gathering dusk. He smiled as he read it: "She was so pleasant."

"Here her grandfather lays."

"Does he?"

"Yes. And here," she added as they went on, "lays Schwable's boy."

She continued the recital until they reached the door of the church.

"Do you want to go in and see it?" she asked. "I come here onct with Elephena," she added as they entered the old country house-of-worship with its high pulpit, high-backed seats, and very old reed-organ. "It's the only church I ever was in."

They strolled up the aisle, and Sabina pointed out its peculiarities.

"That's where the preacher stands," she informed him, pointing to the pulpit. "And there"—directing his attention to the collection-basket that stood on the pulpit stairs—"is what they pass round and everyone puts a cent in. The people sets on them benches. Here," she added, opening a door which led to the gallery that ran around three sides of the room, "is where the stairs go up."

He followed her as she led the way to the gallery.

"It's dark, ain't?" She pushed back a shutter at the head of the stairs, and they walked around the gallery to the organ.

"Here the boy must pull to make the organ play," she explained, pointing out the pump. "He gets ten cents a time."

Suddenly, to Acker's startled amazement, Sabina turned and clutched him by the arm, her face pale, her breath coming in short gasps between her parted lips, her eyes wide with hor-ror and with that strange clairvoyant light which had so mystified him. She tried to speak, but could not utter a sound.

"What is it?" cried Acker. "Are you ill, child? What's the matter?"

"I must go home!" Sabina gasped. "Quick! Somepin's happened 'em at home!"

"What do you mean, Sabina?"

"Come on down!" was her answer, as she groped toward the narrow stairway.

"Give me your hand, or you will fall," Acker said, thinking by firmness of tone to overcome her hysterical fright.

She suffered him to guide her down the stairs and out into the air.

"Leave us hurry!" she urged piteously, and he was almost obliged to run to keep pace with her. He felt himself grow cold with a strange sense of some unseen danger.

"Oh, 'Gustus," she half sobbed, not slackening her pace, "I seen the Face again—the Face that always means trouble!"

"*What* face? I don't understand what—"

"Wait till we get home. I can't talk now!"

He urged her no more, but hurried with her through the graveyard and into the woods. The evening shadows were gathering thick among the tall trees.

"Leave me take your hand!" she begged as they entered the dimness of the little forest. "I might—might—see it again!"

He clasped her hand protectingly and they hastened on. Not another word did either one utter in the ten minutes that passed before they reached the farmhouse.

Sabina snatched her hand from his, and darting through the gate, ran up the board walk and entered the kitchen. Acker followed her rapidly.

No sign of disaster greeted them here. Mrs. Wilt was placidly getting Sammy and Melinda ready for bed, a ceremony always performed in the kitchen; Aunt Susanna was sitting by the window knitting, and Levi was nodding over the *Weekly Intelligencer.*

Sabina stood on the threshold, her hand pressed upon her breast. Acker looked into her eyes to see whether this reassuring domestic picture had not dissipated their strange fire. But it burned there more hotly than before.

"Where was you so long, Biney?" her mother inquired, glancing up from her task. "Why, what's the matter of you?"

"I think!" cried Aunt Susanna. "How you look, Biney! Your hair is all strubbled! And your skirt hangs so out!"

Levi, aroused by their voices, sat up to hear the girl's answer.

"Where's Aaron?" she gasped.

"He's went over to see if he couldn't see Elephena. Oh, Biney!" Mrs. Wilt rose in alarm, and Levi, too, came quickly forward.

"Somepin' 's happened to him!" she sobbed. "I—seen—the Face again! Somepin' 's happened to Aaron!"

"Biney! Biney!" her father said soothingly, though his tone betrayed his own alarm. It was manifest, indeed, that Sabina's fright had infected the whole family, Acker himself not excepted. "Come on in and set," her father urged. "You'll be sick if you leave yourself—"

"Pop," she interrupted in a low voice that thrilled with its note of tragic dignity, "hitch up and go after Aaron! Somepin' has happened!"

Without another word, Levi stumbled out of the kitchen and disappeared into the stable.

The mother, looking anxious and distressed, returned to Sammy and Melinda, and Aunt Susanna nervously resumed her knitting.

"Sabina," urged Acker, "come outside and tell me what all this means."

The girl, still white and now almost apathetic, allowed herself to be led out of doors, and they sat down side by side on the porch steps.

In a voice so low he had now and then to bring his ear close to her lips, she told him of the grim vision that came now and then to haunt her, and of the calamity it inevitably foretold.

"One night, a year back a'ready, when I was off on visiting my Auntie Rebecca over in Cocalico township, I had a dream of seein' such a ugly face of a man—so wicked-like! When I come awake, I couldn't remember none of my dream, but just that ugly face. And I knowed, as certain as if Christ had tole it to me, that somebody at home was in trouble. I was to stay at Auntie Rebecca's a week, and this here was only the third day, but nothin' would do me, after my dream, but to go right straight on home. I tole Auntie Rebecca about my dream and the Face, and she didn't put much credit on it. She sayed I was hystericky. But nothin' she nor anyone sayed stopped me. I come home. And sure enough, here Melinda had fell in the well and was nearly drownded! All that night while I was dreamin' of the Face, the doctor and pop and mom and Aunt Susanna was workin' to keep Melinda alive!"

She stopped abruptly and shivered. It did not need the straightforward simplicity of her recital to carry conviction to Acker's mind; for had he not himself witnessed the manifestation of her strange power in the episode of their drive on the day of his arrival? He began to grow oddly uncomfortable, and he tried in vain to throw off a vague feeling as of some impending disaster.

"But how about this evening?" he inquired. "It was not a dream this time."

"Since that time a year back," she answered, "I seen the Face twict wery plain, onct when Aaron he speaked to me he was goin' to marry Elephena Schwenkfelders; and the other time when we was drivin' home from fetchin' you. I seen it dim onct—" she paused and colored painfully.

"Well, Biney?" he urged.

"I don't like to tell about that time," she faltered, "when I seen it dim. But here this evening"—with a little catch in her voice—"just as I was standin' there with you in the gallery, I seen it wery sudden—as plain before me as life! And then I had that same feelin' of bein' so sure as if Christ had spoke that somepin' was wrong at home! And now I know it must be Aaron."

Acker rose from the porch, and going indoors, came out with a shawl which he laid about her shoulders. "I am afraid you will make yourself ill," he said as he sat down beside her. Her white, fear-stricken face, in the dim light of the summer evening, made him think of the face of the Mater Dolorosa. Yet she was not so absorbed

in her trouble but that she blushed with pleasure at his solicitous attention.

What did it all mean, he wondered? Was the
girl a psychic medium—a clairvoyant?

"I can't think where first I could of saw that
face, 'Gustus," the girl went on, finding comfort in talking to Acker. "To be sure, it might
have been one of them faces in the circus
parade I seen onct in there at Lancaster. Us
Amish we don't uphold to circuses, but when
me and Ulmer was in town on market-day onct
and the parade come along, we stood in the
front ranks, *too,* to see what was going on; and
my conscience troubled me a heap fur lookin'
on at such a worldly scen'ry as that there. Do
you think mebbe I seen the Face that day and
that it comes back to me in my dreams? Mebbe
Gawd sends it to me fur a punishment fur to
trouble me because I looked at the parade
that day."

"No, child, no. There was nothing wrong in
your looking at the parade; and that is not the
way we are punished for our sins. Of course I
don't know whether you saw the Face that day,
or *ever* saw it actually. It's queer enough. Does
Ulmer know of your—of the Face?"

"Yes. He don't like it. He says it near makes
him not want to marry me sometimes. That

much he don't like it! Well," she sighed tremulously, "I don't like it neither. Who *would?*"

There was a long silence, and then Mrs. Wilt and Aunt Susanna joined them on the porch; and the four sat up to await Levi's return long past their usual hour for retiring.

"Levi could of rode to Elephena's and back home again before this," murmured Mrs. Wilt, as the clock in the kitchen struck ten.

"Elephena's mom she's like a crazy person when she's awful worked up," was Aunt Susanna's cheerful suggestion.

So they anxiously speculated while they waited.

It was some time after eleven that the sound of distant wheels on the highroad brought them all to their feet with pale faces and fast-beating hearts. Acker found himself strangely stirred, not only in his sympathy for the others, but in his growing conviction that Sabina's premonition was about to come true.

The approaching vehicles were quickly recognized as belonging to Levi and Aaron, and as the horses drew up to the gate, and the anxious watchers hurried forward, they saw that Aaron's buggy was driven by their neighbor, Pete Zook, while Aaron, seated in his father's carriage, was leaning against his shoulder, his eyes closed, his face white and wan, his left coat sleeve hanging loose, and his left arm wrapped in bandages.

Levi jumped out of his buggy and called out in high, excited tones: "Elephena's mom she up't and throwed boiling water at Aaron, and it burnt his arm and leg bad. But the Lord didn't leave it go in his face. The doctor's been workin' with him over to Sam Buckart's for a couple of hours. He's got him easier now, fur all he's wonderful sick. The doctor give him *morphine* to stop the pain. Sam Buckart he insisted us stayin' all night, but Aaron he wouldn't have it that way—he sayed he was good enough to come along home. But he's still wonderful weak from the shock, the doctor says."

Acker helped the father carry Aaron into the house and upstairs to his room, followed by his distressed and frightened mother, and by Aunt Susanna, bearing a lamp and delivering a volley of her maxims: "'Happy who is single yet, sad who is engaged.' Yes, yes. 'As we make it, so we have it.' If Aaron wouldn't keep comp'ny outside an Amish family, he wouldn't come by such luck. As the sayin' is, 'Hadn't you climbed up, you wouldn't of fell down.'"

As Acker went to his room that night, he saw Sabina sitting on a chair in the kitchen, her hands folded in her lap in unwonted idleness, the tears falling softly down her cheeks, her great eyes staring before her with a look that made his heart ache.

CHAPTER SIX

SABINA BECOMES AMBITIOUS

AARON'S INJURIES WERE NOT SERIOUS, AND IN A few days he was up and about again.

While Acker's observation of Sabina led to no clue as to the mystery of her personality, it showed him the deeply troubled mind of the girl with regard to her brother. He saw how furtively she watched Aaron in the days that followed, and how coldly Aaron repulsed her piteous attempts at propitiating him. The youth was in dire straits with his Elephena, and Sabina's indifference to Ulmer was the cause of it. Aaron would not forgive his sister until she was ready to make the only amends possible. He would not eat the dishes she expressly prepared, he would not touch the newspaper she brought to him, or take the chair she pushed

toward him, or notice in any way her many little remorseful attentions.

She, meantime, wore a face of suffering that
clearly betrayed her inward struggle. Nothing
could lift the cloud of sadness on her young
face save one thing which Acker would hardly
allow himself to see—a word or look of kindness from him. That was her only compensation
for the alienation of her lover and the conse-
quent trouble she caused her brother.

Because of his interest in the phenomenon of
her clairvoyant power, he welcomed her com-
panionship on his evening walks and occasional
drives, too much absorbed in his study of the
girl to consider whither such intimacy would
lead them, how dangerous to the peace of mind
of both. With all his efforts, he could not discover the secret of her power. In every other
respect she seemed commonplace enough, with
perhaps a bit less apathy than the rest of the
family and a little more intelligence.

Her occasional comments on his sketches did
not suggest that she was gifted with any latent
genius for art.

"How do you come over that Scripture," she
once asked him, "where says we ain't to make
no images of nothing in earth or heaven or hell
or the ocean yet?"

She was shelling peas on the back porch, while he, sitting beside her, sketched the nearby orchard.

"I'm afraid I'm not a good enough theologian to tell you, Sabina."

"But don't you feel a little conscientious when you take and do things where Scripture says hadn't ought to be did?"

"There are different ways of interpreting the Scriptures, Sabina, even when one does use them as an infallible guide."

These words, he saw, were quite "too high" for her comprehension. She did not venture to comment on them. She leaned forward and glanced at his canvas.

"Is that there a sheep, mebbe, you're drawin'?"

"No, Sabina, it's a tree," he answered cheerfully.

She regarded it critically. "It does look some like a tree, too," she granted, and he could not decide whether her tone was meant to be encouraging or pitying.

"When the sketch is finished I hope this tree will resemble a sheep less than you now think it does, Biney."

"Yes, anyhow!" she said fervently.

"Would you like to learn to draw?"

"I couldn't waste my time," she shook her head. "What good to a body is a picture of a thing? When you're got the trees and sky all around you, what's the use wastin' time makin' pictures of 'em? It ain't worth while."

"But don't you sometimes see pictures that give you pleasure?"

She shook her head again. "I always thought, when I seen 'em, it ain't worth while."

Acker felt an unreasoning depression at the dreary matter-of-factness of this outlook, so characteristically Amish.

He occasionally lent her books, and though she had never formed the habit of reading, she devoured them eagerly and with more under-standing than he had given her credit for. Her father fondly thought her very "smart."

The time was now approaching for his neces-sary return to Lancaster; and he could not help seeing how Sabina began to droop and grow pale, and it was impossible for him to escape the conclusion that she was grieving at the thought of his going away.

"Surely this isn't going to be a tragic matter to her," he tried to convince himself, with a strange sinking of his heart. "I'll advise her, before I go, to be kinder to Ulmer."

He seized the opportunity to do so the next time he found himself alone with her, which was one evening about a week before his expected departure. She had come out to him in the orchard, where he had been strolling about ever since the early supper. Somehow she was always near him whenever her work allowed her a free moment.

"Finished your work?" he asked.

"Yes," she nodded. "I'm through all, now. I hunted the eggs, too, after I milked. I'd ruther hunt the eggs than dry the dishes fur Aunt Susanna. I'd sooner work out around than in the house, still."

"Sabina," he said, as they walked slowly over the grass under the heavily laden apple trees, "before I leave here, I want to urge you to mend your ways as regards poor Ulmer Popple. That much-slighted youth has my sympathy, Sabina! You ought to try to care for him; I believe you would be so much happier if you did."

He felt that put it lamely; somehow the words did not come easily. He was conscious of a sort of cruelty in uttering them, and of insincerity.

She did not answer at once; and he could not read in her downcast eyes what she thought of his advice. Presently, without looking up, she asked him, in a low voice, "Why do *you* want me to care fur Ulmer Popple?"

"For the reason I gave you—I think you would be happier."

"But why?"

"He is the best fellow about here. You acknowledge that yourself."

"But what makes *you* care if I'm happy or no?"

"Aren't we very good friends, you and I? Of course I want to see you happy."

"Are *you* happy, 'Gustus?" She lifted her eyes and looked into his as she asked the question.

"I'm usually too busy to stop to consider that, Sabina. On the whole, I think I'm pretty well satisfied with things."

"Ain't there any things you want where you ain't got?"

"Lots of things. I'm too poor for comfort and—"

"*You* poor?" she repeated incredulously. "When you have time to spend without workin' and can wear your best suit every day!"

"But I've been working all summer," he assured her; "I've been sketching four hours a day this whole blessed month; and my best suit is the only suit I have!"

"But sketchin' ain't *work*."

"It's the hardest kind of work, Sabina."

"Well, what else do you want where you ain't got—besides money?"

"Oh—after a while, I'll want a mate. But that's a blessing in store for me. Plenty of time for that."

"How long are you goin' to wait before you think about gettin' married and settlin'?"

"I'll think about it as soon as I see the proper lady."

"Ain't you never seen her yet?" she asked wistfully.

The simplicity of her candor fairly hurt him.

"No," he answered, taking refuge behind a very matter-of-fact tone, "I have not. I am sure that when I do I shall recognize her instantly."

He was not sure of anything of the sort, but he thought it best to disabuse her mind of any faintest suspicion that possibly *she* might be his Joan.

"But you, Sabina," he continued; "the sooner you reconcile yourself—I mean the sooner you decide to be to Ulmer the sweet wife you are destined to be—"

"I don't feel near so much fur gettin' married to Ulmer towards what I felt there fur a while, before—before—A girl hadn't ought to marry a man unlest she can like him better'n anyone else in the world," said Sabina, doggedly.

"And that's the way you ought to like Ulmer."

"But—I like—another one—better," she faltered piteously.

"Oh, you only imagine that!" Acker put in cheerfully, but there was a hurt in his own soul that he would not and could not analyze.

"I've conceited to do somepin'," she abruptly announced.

He looked at her in some apprehension.

"I've conceited I'd ask pop to send me to the Millersville Normal fur a year—to get me more *educated.*"

"Whatever put that in your head, Sabina?"

"Don't *you* think I need to be more *educated* than what I am a'ready, 'Gustus?" she anxiously inquired.

"That depends upon circumstances. You have education enough to be Ulmer's wife. A woman doesn't want to know *too* much more than her husband."

"It ain't fur to be Ulmer's wife I want to be more *educated.*"

"What for, then?"

"Since I am born I lived on the farm; I'm tired livin' on the farm onct. I want to see how other ones live; and I want to learn books better."

"It might do you a great deal of good to go to the Normal School for a year," he heartily agreed. "But I think you will come back to the farm quite contented to live here for the rest of your days."

"You think I won't like the world's ways?"

"Have any of your people ever been contented in breaking away from the Amish way of life? Your father tells me that the few who have tried it always return to their own settlements and their old life."

"I'm goin' to see onct, anyway, if pop'll leave me go. He won't want to; but if I plague him a good bit, mebbe he will, fur all."

When, a little while later, they went into the lighted kitchen, he was struck with the pallor of the girl's face.

She did not stop to speak to any of the assembled family, but took her lamp and went directly upstairs.

"Biney must be some tired. As a general, she ain't fur goin' to bed so early," said her mother.

"Since 'Gustus is here we're all takin' to late hours," remarked Levi. "It's near nine every night till we get to bed!"

"Yes, and it wastes the coal-oil to set up so late," put in Aunt Susanna. "That's a good sayin', 'If you save in time you have it in need.'"

CHAPTER SEVEN

LEVI AIRS HIS VIEWS

ACKER DID NOT BELIEVE THAT THE ECONOMICAL Levi would consent to put up the money for a year's schooling and board at Millersville for his daughter. But there was an aspect of the case of which he was not aware until Levi told him of it.

It was in the leisure that came to the farmer on Sunday afternoon that Acker had a chance to speak to him on the subject and plead Sabina's cause, as she had asked him to do. He found Levi alone on the porch, laboriously perusing the *Weekly Intelligencer*, the only mental exercise in a literary way, except an occasional conning of the Bible, in which the Amishman ever indulged.

"I don't take this here paper no more," Levi announced as Acker sat down beside him on the porch step. "Next market-day, I go to the *Intelligencer* office and tell 'em I'm quittin' their paper."

"Don't you like its politics?"

"I don't bother about them politics. It ain't that."

Acker waited to be enlightened.

"I'm tryin' the *New Ery.*"

"You think you'll like its views better?"

"Och, no. It kin have what views it wants. They don't bother me any."

"The *New Era* cheaper?" Acker hazarded.

"No, it ain't. But look a-here. Them *Intelligencer* folks they print their paper on such little sheets we can't use 'em to cover our cupboard shelfs still. And the paper's so thin that we can't make it do to cover our apple-butter crocks. What do *I* want of such a paper where can't be used fur shelfs or apple-butter crocks? I'm stoppin' at their office next market-day to read 'em off a piece of my mind fur sendin' me such a paper. And then I'm tryin' the *New Ery.*"

Acker lost himself in a picture of the long-haired, hooked-and-eyed Levi in the newspaper office, declaiming his displeasure because the paper couldn't be used to cover cupboards and apple-butter jars.

But noticing, presently, that Levi was growing drowsy from his heavy Sunday dinner, he hastened to remark: "I want to speak to you about Sabina's going to Millersville."

"Now I look at it this here way," Levi ponder-ously reasoned, laying off his propositions one after another on his thick fingers: "While my childern's under age and has no money of their own, they have to do what I say. But when they come twenty-one (if it's a boy) or eighteen (if she's a girl) and has got money of their own saved till then—then I don't say to 'em, 'You got to do that' or 'You got to do this.' While they're under age and I'm supportin' 'em, I'm their boss; but when they're twenty-one, or eighteen, it's their own affairs what they do with their money or where they go. Aaron he sayed to me when he was sixteen, now he'd like more schoolage. 'Well,' I says, 'when you're twenty-one and have got the money, you dare go to school all you want. But it's more impor-tant you learn first to work and earn your livin'.' I uphold to learnin' practical work first," con-tinued Levi. "If we sent childern away to school when they're young, they grow away from the farm in their feelin', mebbe, and foller after the world's ways. And we want our childern to settle down near us to be farmers or the wives of farmers."

"Sabina is eighteen. Are you, then, going to let her have her own way and send her to Millersville?"

"I sayed to her that I thought it was a foolish idea. 'But you're of age,' I says, 'and have got your own money, and it ain't fur me to say you haven't dare to do what you want with it, fur all I adwise you ag'in' wastin' it goin' to school, when you might save it up ag'in' the time you're married,' I says to her."

"Sabina has her own money?"

"Her butter-and-egg money. Since she was thirteen a'ready, I paid her fur churnin' and milkin' and keepin' the chickens, and she's got all that there saved up—about four hundred dollars. I ast her what *practical* use to her was any more education than what she's got? And she says she'd mebbe come back and teach the district school. I adwised Biney ag'in' it, fur all I sayed she has dare to do what she wants. 'Look a-here,' I sayed to her, 'you'll mebbe be wantin' to get married to a town feller if you go in there to school!' 'Well,' she says, 'mebbe I will.' 'But, Biney,' I tole her, 'them marriages ain't happy.' The city ladies has tole me in there at Lancaster market a'ready how they hadn't saw their mister this couple days back, the mister bein' off on business or what. A country wife couldn't stand that, they're so used to havin' their man with 'em all the time. It would be too lonely. Why, Naomi wouldn't leave me go off for one day without her along—nor I wouldn't *want* to, neither."

"What did Sabina say to your warning?" Acker asked.

"She sayed she'd ruther see a man she liked *onct* a week than see one she didn't care for every day, still. I'm afraid"—Levi shook his head—"it ain't goin' to do Biney no good. I ain't spoke nothin' to Naomi yet about Biney's wantin' to get more *educated*. She'll worry wonderful. I'm tellin' her though, today mebbe. Biney says fur *me* to tell her mom."

Acker was impressed with the fact that the mother's consent was not deemed necessary; that she was not even consulted until the whole thing was settled.

He found himself idly wondering what proverb Aunt Susanna would fit to the occasion, and how Ulmer Popple would receive the news of Biney's aspirations after learning.

CHAPTER EIGHT

ULMER AND SABINA

IT WAS ARRANGED THAT SABINA WAS TO GO TO Millersville on the day of Acker's departure. He was invited to be her escort on the New Holland trolley and to put her on the Millersville car at Lancaster.

He was not above hoping that none of his acquaintances would see him acting as escort to the grotesquely clad Amish girl. It would be an unusual sight, for the Amish, more than all the other sects of the county, withdraw themselves from all contact with "the world's people."

A soft radiance of happy expectation seemed to surround Sabina in the week preceding her departure, clouded only occasionally when confronted by Aaron's countenance of gloom, or when she met her mother's wistful gaze.

Acker speculated a good deal as to how she would fit in with life at the Normal School. She would be an oddity among the students; she would be ridiculed, perhaps, because of her outlandish costume; she had never been away from home, and she was shy—no doubt she would suffer agonies of homesickness among strangers and those of alien ways. Would she derive sufficient benefit from the experience to make up for the inevitable suffering? He would not admit even to himself the conviction, in the background of his consciousness, that it was her feeling for him which inspired her ambitions and which would sustain her through all the trials of her new life.

"Are you going to say good-by to Ulmer?" he asked her.

"It'll soon get put out all over the Meetin' that I'm goin', and when Ulmer he hears it I don't know if he *will* come over to give me good-by."

"And sha'n't you care whether he comes or not?"

"He can come if he wants," she said guardedly.

"I am hoping your separation from him will make you appreciate him, Sabina."

She shook her head as she lifted her eyes to his. "No; the more I see of other ones, the more I don't feel fur gettin' married to Ulmer."

This was approaching dangerous ground, and Acker beat a hasty retreat.

That same evening, as he was starting out for his customary stroll, Sabina—who for several evenings past had missed her coveted walk with him, inasmuch as, with conscientious purpose, he had gone off each time before her work was finished and had thus avoided her— now came up to him as he was stepping out on the kitchen porch.

With just a nod, he put on his hat and started down the porch steps.

"'Gustus!"

There was a trembling appeal in her voice as she stopped him.

"Well?"

"I'm through all. Can I—can I come with?"

"But, Sabina—Ulmer might be over."

"Don't you want me with, 'Gustus?"

The hopeless melancholy in her voice and look was too much for him. He turned and laid his hand on her shoulder as she stood in the doorway.

"Of course I want you, child. But I have no right to take you away from Ulmer."

"Ulmer ain't got no rights over me. Oh!" She started and drew back, but not before Ulmer Popple, Suddenly appearing around a corner of the porch, had caught sight of a picture that made him bristle aggressively.

He stopped short and glared.

Acker mentally kicked himself for being caught in a position that would seem to justify the other's jealousy.

"Good evening," he said pleasantly. "Biney was rather expecting you this evening."

"Oh, she was, was she?" Ulmer retorted in a tone that suggested clenched fists. "She wasn't expecting me just this minute, I guess! No, I guess not! I give her and you an unexpected surprise *this* time; say not?"

"If you come over to see me, Ulmer," Sabina interposed, "come on in, then. 'Gustus he's goin' out walkin'."

"And you was goin' with, I guess! I wouldn't put it a-past neither of yous!"

"No; Biney was going to stop at home and wait for you," Acker gravely reassured him. "She thought you might be over, perhaps. Good-by." He lifted his hat, turned abruptly, and walked down the board walk to the gate.

Ulmer's belligerent gaze followed him for a moment, then turned back to Sabina. The girl's eyes were wistfully watching the retreating figure of Acker.

Now Ulmer Popple had never, before the last few weeks, conceived the possibility of such a thing as that he should have a rival. His sway over the feminine hearts of the Meeting had always been undisputed. He had only to choose, not woo, the girl he wanted to marry. It had never occurred to him that it was necessary to make himself acceptable to the lady of his approval, his sole idea being that it was her business to make herself acceptable to him. That was the view the girls themselves seemed to take of it, too—all of them except the one girl to whom he felt irresistibly attracted. She actually did not seem to think as much of him as she did of another! And he was confronted by the necessity of humbling himself to please *her*, instead of graciously accepting her grateful efforts to please him—a reversal of the proper order of things that bewildered him.

"Will you go buggy-ridin' with me this evening, Biney?" he demanded. "I got my buggy out back. I heerd you was goin' to Millersville Normal yet! I couldn't hardly believe it! I come over to see onct if it's so. Come on out ridin' with me, and you tell me then."

"I don't care if I do, Ulmer," she answered, without eagerness. "I'll go fetch my bonnet."

"Now," he asked, as they drove out of the stable-yard, "where shall we go to?"

"I'd like to drive up through Zook's woods, Ulmer; that's a pretty ride."

He looked at her sharply. "That's no place to ride to. You just think that there dude's walkin' up there—he *sayed* he was goin' fur a walk. Mebbe you was goin' to walk along with him, like I sayed, if I hadn't of come over?" he darkly suggested, though he obediently turned the horse in the direction of Zook's woods.

"Mebbe I was," answered Biney, softly.

Ulmer looked discouraged. What arguments could be used against such complacency?

"*Well*," he declared presently, "the talk is around here that you and him is keepin' comp'ny. Now look a-here, Biney! I'm a man, and I know the world's ways better'n you do, seein' you're nothin' but a female; and I uphold that this here dude is either crazy or he's a black-eyed willain—one of them two."

"His eyes is blue," said Sabina.

"Willains near all has black eyes. You didn't look good at him, I guess."

"You think!" said Biney, ironically.

"Well, I kin prove you he's a willain or either he's crazy. Elephena she tole me some things about that feller. She says he sayed, when he was settin' on the porch, onct, how he seen Things in the sky—a *dipper* yet! . . . A big dipper and a little dipper! And a *coffin!* Job's coffin, he sayed he seen! He's daft—that's what!"

"Och, Ulmer, you're dumn! That's astronomy, that learns you all about the stars, and the moon, and them."

"Well, Biney Wilt! And you'd believe a thing like that just because that feller sayed it? You're just stubborn-headed."

"You think!" Biney tossed her head.

"I think he's crazy *and* a liar! It's him that's got you to think you'd like to spend your money goin' to Millersville Normal. And onct he gets you in there at Lancaster"—Ulmer almost choked in his hot anger—"*he* knows what he'll do you!"

"He won't do me nothin', Ulmer!" Biney said indignantly.

"Yes, he will! And you bein' only a female, you don't see through it like what I do, bein' a male. He's got you that fooled with him you'd believe anything he says. But you mind, Biney, if you ain't sorry, someday, you went on his words and left your home to go out into the wide world along with him! That kind of feller *he* wouldn't marry no Amish girl! It stands to reason. And if he ain't goin' to marry you, what fur does he come out here enticin' you off of me, and takin' you to meetin', and out walkin', and settin' up with you—and persuadin' you to go to town with him, and waste your good money that there way, when you might have it fur your weddin'? Do you know what he does all them things fur, Biney? Because he's a sharper! That's why!"

As he spoke there crept into the girl's heart the recollection of the bewilderment she had experienced on the day of Acker's arrival— when, dimly, she had seen the evil Face, but so indefinitely, so unlike all its previous and subsequent aspects, that she had not been sure that it conveyed its customary warning.

"I tell you he didn't put me up to goin' to the Normal, Ulmer," she protested, "whether you think I'm only a female or whether you don't! And if mom and pop don't mistrust to send me along in town with him to take care of me—"

"*Him* to take care of you yet!" Ulmer's sarcasm was profound.

"If *they* don't mistrust to leave him take care of me," Biney resumed, "I guess you needn't, Ulmer."

They had reached Zook's woods, and as they drove in under the big dark trees, there in the path ahead of them was Acker, strolling leisurely along, his trained eye noting with keen pleasure each shadowy vista as it opened up before him.

Sabina had the grace to color guiltily as she saw him. She sank back limply in the white wagon when Ulmer turned his accusing eyes upon her.

Acker did not turn at the sound of the wheels, but merely stepped out of the road to the grass and walked on. Not until they were passing him did he look up, and even then his glance met Ulmer's instead of Biney's as he lifted his hat.

Ulmer sneered at this unnecessary ceremony, as they drove on.

"I guess you like them dude ways of hisn," he said—"tippin' his hat and them."

"I cert'nly do," Sabina shamelessly acknowledged.

"You'd mebbe like *me* to go round tippin' my hat to females, aint?"

"It wouldn't come wery handy, tippin' such a wide-brimmed Amish hat. But if the Amish hats wasn't so big, I think them ways is nice."

"You'll be comin' home from the Normal wearin' the world's garb!" Ulmer presaged darkly.

Sabina offered no protest or denial.

"Say, Biney! Tell me, onct fur all, what you're up to anyhow."

"I ain't up to nothin' but to get more *educated* than what I am. Further than that I ain't lookin' ahead any."

"Tell me—honest to Gawd—if there ain't nothin' between you and this here 'Gustus."

"Not so fur, there ain't."

"But you're countin' on there bein' somepin' till you're got your education a'ready, heh?"

"I sayed I ain't lookin' ahead any," Sabina obstinately repeated.

Further assurance than this, Ulmer's utmost efforts failed to extract from her. During all the rest of the drive he strove with her, begging her not to go away; not to waste her time and money in such useless folly; not to trust the "black-eyed stranger" (in spite of Sabina's repeated assurances that the stranger's eyes were blue), but to stay at home and give herself to him.

Sabina softened and grew kinder as he became humbler and pleaded his cause less arbitrarily. But he failed utterly to gain from her any promise of faithfulness to him during her devious wanderings in the world's ways.

"We'll see onct, till I come back, how I feel. I ain't passin' my promise now."

"And I guess you'll be expectin' me to wait fur you all this time, instead of goin' and marryin' another one, like I'd have the right to do!"

"I ain't expectin' nothin', Ulmer. You have dare to do what you want."

"Mebbe you'll be only too glad, till you come home, to have me—or any other feller that would have *you*."

"I don't know, *I'm* sure, how I'll feel till then."

"Well, I ain't promisin' to wait till you get good and ready to say 'yes.' If I make up my mind fur Elephena, I'm gettin' married to her. And you can be a old maid!"

"All right, Ulmer."

Ulmer's eye searched her face in the gathering dusk, to see whether such indifference to her own best interests could possibly be sincere.

He could read nothing therein that gave him any hope.

CHAPTER NINE

ON THE FRONT PORCH

SINCE THE ADVENT OF THE BOARDER, THE WILTS had quite fallen into the habit of sitting on the front porch for a half-hour before going to bed. With the exception of Aaron, who held aloof from every one these days, they were all gathered there this evening, when Acker came back from his stroll and Sabina returned from her drive.

The family had taken hope from this drive, thinking it highly probable that Sabina would come home having been persuaded to give up her worldly desire for more education, for the manifestly better fate of becoming Ulmer Popple's wife.

This hope, however, was nipped in the bud as Ulmer let her climb out of the buggy at the gate and then drove away at his fastest pace.

"That shows they ain't fixed it up," sighed Aunt Susanna to Acker. "Or else Ulmer would've got out and come along in. I wonder what makes Biney act so dumn! She sayed to me today she thought Ulmer wasn't enough intelligent to suit her—that he never talked nothin' *interestin'* that way. 'Ach, Biney,' I says to her, 'there's a sayin' just fits you, One ass calls another Long-Ear. And look a-here,' I says, 'you mind the sayin', Two heads is better'n one—if one is a cabbage-head. Biney,' I says, 'if Ulmer ain't just so smart as some, A blind hog sometimes finds an acorn, too; and Ulmer he's smart enough to make money. All the Popples is.'"

Sabina came up the board walk and sat down on the porch at Acker's side.

"Did you give Ulmer good-by?" her father asked, in a tone that was meant to be casual. He was holding small Melinda on his knee as he slowly rocked in the big painted rocking chair.

"Yes," was Sabina's non-committal reply.

Levi looked disappointed and Mrs. Wilt sighed audibly.

Biney stirred uneasily tinder the growing family gloom.

"I suppose," Acker remarked cheerfully, "by the time I come to see you all again—if you will

be so good as to let me come next summer—
Elephena and Aaron will be married and in
their own home. And Sabina will have returned
and been married to Ulmer; and perhaps she
will invite me to take tea with her at her own
table. Eh, Sabina?"

Sabina bent her eyes upon her lap and did
not answer at once, and as Acker saw the
tumultuous heaving of her bosom he realized
how his words had stabbed her. And suddenly
he was possessed with a most unaccountable
desire to take the girl in his arms and comfort
her. He was quite astounded at the depth of
his feelings.

CHAPTER TEN

Sabina Tastes of "the World"

Sabina's state of mind during the hour's trolley ride from New Holland to Lancaster City was pathetically obvious to Acker as he sat at her side and watched her pretty, sensitive face. Excited and eager for the new life before her, she was at the same time almost ill with remorse for the trouble her going might cause Aaron, and also with fright at the prospect of the many strangers she must meet. He realized with a heaviness at his heart that the only thing that sustained and inspired her in carrying out her determination to go to school was her infatuation for him.

He foresaw the suffering ahead of the poor girl, her homesickness, her loneliness, her disappointed anticipations. And there could be no compensation for her in her work, for she had no fondness for study.

All the way to town he battled with his temptation to go with her from the city out to the school and see her safe in her new home. He knew how glad she would be if he offered to do it, and how grateful. It made him sick to think of abandoning her when they reached Lancaster, letting her face alone, in all her shrinking timidity and ignorance, a new life amid alien people. Yet, all things considered, it seemed the wiser course.

So at Lancaster he put her on the Millersville car, and bade her good-by, resisting with some effort the pleading of her beautiful eyes and the piteous quivering of her lips. His voice he strove to make cheerfully matter-of-fact.

"Don't forget, Sabina, if ever you need me, telephone to me, and I shall be glad to do anything I can for you."

"Yes, 'Gustus," she whispered. "Will you—will you ever come out to see me now and again?"

"I'm afraid you and I will both be too busy for any visiting. But I shall come at once if at any time you need me. Now—good-by, for the present, little girl."

"Good-by, 'Gustus."

Great tears trembled on her lashes, and her fingers clung to his for a moment. He wavered; could he desert her like this, poor child?

The motorman struck his bell.

"Good-by, Biney," he said hastily, and turning away abruptly, he left the car.

"How could I be so brutal, how could I?" he kept asking himself all the way to his boardinghouse.

For the rest of the day he kept himself hard at work, unpacking his books, getting his studio in order, and writing letters, that he might keep from his troubled mind and heart the image of that piteous young face whose helpless appeal he had so stoically resisted. And there was not a day, in the very busy weeks that followed, in which that image did not thrust itself before him.

One night, in an hour of relaxation, as he lounged in his easy chair, he tried to analyze his own feelings.

It was absurd to suppose he could have fallen in love with an ignorant, commonplace Amish girl. It was not, it could not be, *love* which stirred him whenever she was near, and which made him wish for her and think of her so constantly now that she was gone. An animal instinct of attraction? But the highly civilized creature he took himself to be surely did not live on a plane so low that his emotions could be stirred by mere physical allurement independent of any spiritual affinity? What was it, then, that made Biney appeal to him as he did not remember ever to have been appealed to before by any woman—that made her power over him, even in her absence, grow stronger day by day?

It was, he finally decided, that quality which is apparently not necessarily coexistent with such things as mental and moral endowment, social culture, sophistication; a wild, ungrafted fruit of nature that may fall equally upon the country maiden of humble birth or "the daughter of a thousand earls," and which will make itself felt with irresistible power through any environment; that quality which defies all defining, yet which, with clear apprehension of its significance, we name feminine charm. There was nothing more to be said. Biney had that charm preëminently, transcendently; and mankind, of whatever degree or condition, was on its knees at her feet.

Levi came to the Lancaster market every other Saturday, and Acker meant to get up early enough some morning to see him there and inquire after Sabina and all the people at the farm. But a good many Saturdays came and went without his having been able to rouse himself at five o'clock in the morning, which is the inhuman hour at which Pennsylvania markets are opened, even in the dead of winter.

When a month had gone by and he had had no word from any of them, he decided it would prove an easier feat than getting out of his comfortable bed at daybreak to go out to the Millersville school to see Sabina. He knew he ought not to do it. Yet, after debating the matter for some time, he finally temporized by calling up the school by telephone.

The answer from the office came in a feminine voice—a voice that was curiously pleasant and cultured.

"May I speak to the principal?" he asked.

"He is not here. I am his secretary. Will you give me your message?"

"I wanted to inquire about Miss Sabina Wilt. Can you tell me, please, how she is?"

"She is well, I think."

"And how is she getting on?"

"You mean in her studies? Really, I don't know her record."

"I mean, is she contented and happy?"

"I am not acquainted with Miss Wilt. Shall I call her to the phone?"

"If you will be so kind."

After a few moments the same voice said: "Miss Wilt is here, but she says she can't speak through the phone. She asks me to talk for her. She wants to know whether it is Mr. Augustus Acker who is talking."

"Yes. I merely wish to learn whether she is well, and is she homesick? How is she getting on?"

A moment's silence, and then the secretary spoke: "Miss Wilt says she is well, but very lonesome."

"Eh?"

"She says I shall say she is particularly lonesome on Saturday evenings."

Acker remembered that this was beau-night among her kin.

"How does she like her school life?" he asked.

"She says the lessons are very hard. And she misses her people."

"Does she intend to stay?"

"She thinks she will try to stay until the term is over at Christmas—if she possibly can. She says if she could see a friend sometimes—on Saturday nights," said the secretary, evidently talking from dictation, "she could stand it better."

"Yes? Well, tell her, please, I am glad she is well, and that she must call on me if she needs me."

"She says, Can you come out to see her some Saturday night?"

"I am so busy—"

"Mr. Acker—may I take the liberty? I advise you to come," came the secretary's voice, in a significant tone.

"Eh? Why?"

"You will see for yourself when you do come."

"Well, tell Sabina, then, I shall be out next Saturday night."

"I will. Good-by."

She rang him off, and he stood committed to his promise.

What had been the meaning of that significant tone in which he had been advised to come? No doubt it meant that Sabina was pining with homesickness and needed to be comforted. He would have to go, since he had promised.

On Saturday evening, when he rang the doorbell of the great school building, it was Sabina herself who opened the door to him.

"'Gustus!" she breathed ecstatically as he took her hand and clasped it, her face radiant with the happiness of seeing him, her bosom rising and falling tumultuously, her eyes swimming in light. There was no pallor, no drooping, woebegone aspect, such as he had expected. But the helpless betrayal of her joy in meeting him struck him as almost more pathetic, and thrilled him strangely.

"I seen you from the window. I watched every car comin' since half-past six a'ready."

She led the way through the wide hall to the great flight of uncarpeted stairs, and as he followed her, he realized what, at a first glance into her shining countenance, he had been diverted from seeing, that her figure had lost its girlish roundness and that her clothes hung upon her limply.

"Let's go upstairs and set in a classroom, 'Gustus," she suggested eagerly.

"Why not in this reception room?" he inquired, as they passed an open door.

"Oh, 'Gustus, I don't never set in them rooms. They're too grand and too much after the world. I don't never set nowheres in this house but in a classroom or in my own bedroom. I feel a little conscientious about it, 'Gustus."

They reached a recitation-room on the second floor, and when she pressed a button in the wall to turn on the electric light, it was revealed to be sufficiently barren and cheerless, in its furniture of wooden benches, platform, and desk, to satisfy even the conscience of an Amish girl.

"You have grown thinner, Sabina," he remarked as they sat down on one of these hard benches. "I don't like to see you so thin. I'm afraid you're not well."

"It ain't that. But—it don't go just so good here," she said, the radiance dying out of her face, the bright color fading from her cheeks, and a heavy sadness stealing over her like a mantle. "I'm so wonderful lonesome. I'm so lonesome I can't eat or sleep. I can't home myself here, 'Gustus."

"But, my child, that will never do," he protested, seeing now that she looked wretchedly ill. "You must either go home, or you must conquer your low spirits. You are injuring yourself."

She looked down at the hands clasped in her lap, and as Acker followed her glance, he saw how thin those hands had grown, and at the same time how smooth and white in their freedom from toil.

"I thought, 'Gustus," she murmured, "you'd be out to see me now and again. Mebbe you can't spare the quarter car-fare to come out; say not?" she asked timidly.

"It's the time I can't spare, Sabina. I am so busy. Haven't you a roommate?"

"No. I had one. But she put a fancy rug on the floor, and two gilt-framed pictures she hung up yet. It made me feel some conscientious to be givin' my countenance to such wain things, so I turned the rug and the pictures every time I come in the room to sit, so's I wouldn't see 'em. And so she ast the preceptress to leave her room with another one. So now I'm alone. Ach, sometimes I have homesick so bad, I get up in the nighttime and put on my cap to pray," she said, a sob in her voice.

"Put on your cap to pray?"

"You know," she explained, "us Amish we don't pray with our heads uncovered. So a couple times I put on my cap in the nighttime and prayed to Christ to help me not to—to—"

"To what, Sabina?"

"To bother you any, like I felt fur doin'. Ach, every day I felt fur writin' you a postal card, and astin' you to come to see me onct—or else I'd *have* to give up and go home; and all my money where I paid fur my schoolage up till Christmastime would be wasted!"

"You'd better lose your money than your health," he answered, repressing his impulse to comfort the child with all the tenderness she so evidently craved. Instead, he treated her with the matter-of-fact coolness his better judgment demanded, but which it took all his strength of will to carry out. "My poor little girl! Go home over Sunday, and you'll feel better when you come back."

She shook her head. "I can't spare the money. And I'm afraid I'd feel worse to come back after I'd seen all the folks."

"Do they write to you?"

"Aunt Susanna she wrote me one letter in here. Mom and pop ain't much fur writin'. And Aaron he won't write me."

"How about him and Elephena?"

"Aunt Susanna she says they ain't runnin' together yet." Sabina sighed deeply.

"And Ulmer?"

"Aunt Susanna she wrote that Ulmer and Elephena's wonderful thick together."

"Tut, tut, Biney! You ought to go home."

She looked at him with eyes that revealed her heart-hunger. "No." She shook her head again; and he saw the uselessness of urging her.

"What are your studies, Sabina?" he asked presently.

"I'm in the Preparatory Department. I study United States history and jogafry and physiology (that learns you about your works inside) and grammar (where learns you how to speak correct) and readin' and spellin' and them; all where I learnt at the district school at home, only these here's harder."

"Do you like your teachers?"

"Middlin'," she nodded.

"What is your favorite study, Sabina?"

"Spellin'," she promptly answered.

Acker looked discouraged.

"The history teacher's wonderful smart. She knows the whole book by heart—even the footnotes yet!"

"Yes?"

There was a little silence between them, which Acker presently broke by leaning toward her and asking gravely, "Sabina, have you seen that face again?"

Her cheeks grew a shade paler, and her eyes dilated.

"Not since that night Aaron was hurt, 'Gustus," she answered, moving nearer to him on the bench, her whole look and tone seeming to appeal to him for protection against the mysterious horror that was wont to haunt her.

He was instantly sorry that he had asked the question.

"Perhaps you will never see it again. Don't let us think of it."

"But, 'Gustus, what if I would see it onct while I'm off here alone so far away from the folks! I'd near go crazy!"

"If you sent for me, I would come out here to you at once."

He spoke partly to reassure her, partly because of his interest in her weird psychic experience; but as he saw her pallor give way to a rosy glow, the horror of her eyes soften to a tender delight, and her frightened countenance turn to a look of confident dependence upon him, he feared he had been rash.

To divert her mind from the subject, he began to tell her a little of his own life and work, insofar as he thought she could understand it. He was not given to discussing himself or his affairs, but her eager, thirsty drinking in of his words (to her he was evidently the prince who could not speak without dropping pearls) rather spurred him on to be communicative. To be sure, there were not wanting among his acquaintances and friends many girls who would have given his egotism the same flattering interest and attention; but in this unsophisticated Amish girl there was a sincerity so absolute, a lack of self-consciousness so new in his experience of the fair sex, that, though he was loath to acknowledge it to himself, she held a unique charm for him—such as he had never before found in any woman.

When, at half-past nine o'clock, he was obliged, by the rules of the school, to take his departure, he realized that the evening had been an intense pleasure to him and that he regretted its coming to an end.

Sabina's eyes followed him with passionate longing up to the last glimpse she had of him before he left her at the great front door.

CHAPTER ELEVEN

A POSTAL FROM AARON

ANOTHER MONTH PASSED BY, DURING WHICH Acker resolutely resisted going to see Sabina or communicating with her in any way.

One Saturday morning he managed to look up Levi behind his market-stall in Centre Square and inquire after the family.

Levi appeared mildly pleased to see him. "Naomi asts me near every week did I now see you onct in town. She'll be glad when I tell her 'yes' this time."

"Is everybody well?"

"All but Aaron. He's feelin' so bad he can't work right no more. Ulmer Popple he's in so thick with Elephena; and Elephena's mom she favors Ulmer. Ulmer'll mebbe leave Meetin' and join to the Lutherans. That's what the talk is. Us, we're sorry fur Aaron's feelin's, but we are glad fur his soul that Elephena she'll not lead *him* into the world."

Acker expressed his sympathy, and asked whether they had yet grown accustomed to Sabina's absence.

"No; we can't seem to used ourselfs to her bein' away. One of these here days I'll send her a quarter-dollar out, to come in to Lancaster and ride home with me from market for over Sunday"; and he smiled gently at his own whimsical generosity.

"What's your beets?" asked a woman, wedging her way close to the stall.

"Beets is five cents a bunch," Levi answered.

"I'll see you again when you are not so busy," Acker told him, as he pushed his way through the dense stream of housewives carrying baskets, and made for the middle of the street.

It was but a fortnight later that he was surprised one morning to receive a postal card from Aaron:

Frend, It got put out here how U. popple he was Marrying elephena till nex Week yet. and so i up and went and Got elephena to run Away with Me to our place She is staying here till we get Married nex satrdy aready. she is turned Plain

and is wearing a amish frock of barbara Schna-
bel's where I lent off of barbara for elephena
We was Published in Meeting last sunday that we
would be Married in a Week. Come on along out
with biney for the Wedding on satrdy and oblij
your trew frend

Aaron Wilt

Acker reflected that this invitation was no doubt prompted as much by Aaron's willingness to pay back Ulmer some of the suffering he had endured on his account, as by any friendliness for himself.

An opportunity to see an Amish wedding, and this particular one, was a temptation not to be resisted.

His thoughts dwelt for a time on that unhappy premonition which had come to Sabina when Aaron had first told her of his betrothal to Elephena; and he speculated as to what it might have meant—if it had meant anything; and whether trouble in the shape of Elephena's mother was likely to mar her daughter's wedding day. He wondered at the same time whether he ever would solve the mystery of Sabina's prophetic visions of the Face.

He decided that it would be wiser not to go out on the car with Sabina. When he had telephoned to Millersville and learned what car she expected to take on Friday morning, he told her—through the medium of the secretary with the attractive voice—that he could not get off so early, but would reach the farm sometime in the afternoon.

So each went alone on the long and dreary ride to New Holland.

When Acker arrived at the Wilt farm, the mammoth preparations for the wedding were almost completed, and he was treated to a display of twelve large roasted ducks, three chickens, sixty pounds of roast beef, eighteen large layer-cakes, besides an enormous quantity of small cakes, and fifty large homemade pies. His astonishment upon seeing this great quantity of food brought a lament from Aunt Susanna.

"Yes, this way all us Amish cooks fur weddins," she sighed, "and it's a custom where ought to go off, because the poor wants to make after. And it costs expensive."

"Are there any poor Amish?" Acker asked.

"Not to say just beggars that way. But some rents—their farms ain't paid fur."

As for the bride-elect, Acker saw that while she appeared to be happy in her relations with Aaron, and in having at last settled irrevocably the question of their marriage, she manifested constant uneasiness, as though in dread of an unwelcome visit from her mother.

"Till I'm married onct, I don't feel safe," she told Acker. "I can't think mom'll leave me go without tryin' to get me back."

Levi and Naomi appeared to be reconciled to the match since Elephena had joined Meeting and assumed the garb. Yet that they felt Aaron might have done better, was manifested in Levi's frankly spoken regret, in the very presence of Elephena, that she came to his son without the customary "ausstyer," or dower, and that he himself would therefore have to furnish it. This deficiency on her part was evidently as sore a shame to Elephena as it was a source of dissatisfaction to her prospective father-in-law.

Aunt Susanna, of course, improved the occasion by quoting proverbs to the young couple.

"I don't believe Ulmer will come to the weddin' tomorrow," Mrs. Wilt remarked anxiously to Sabina. "Not just by our invitation to the congregation at meetin'. He'll have to be sent a special invitation; or if he does come, he'll pair off with some other one and not with you," she predicted.

"Well," Sabina conceded, "*I* ain't carin' much."

"Look a-here, Biney Wilt, if you don't watch out," warned Aunt Susanna, "you'll be an old maid yet, and *then* think how you'd feel!"

Sabina was "making the table for supper" while this dialogue was going on, and Acker was sitting by the window, his eyes following her as she moved about the room.

"Is that a more dreadful fate among the Amish than among the world's people: to be an old maid?" Acker asked.

"We have wery seldom single people in the country," Mrs. Wilt explained. "It looks awful bad not to get married out here—like as if you was such a dopplig housekeeper no man would have you."

The woman's childlike eyes fairly dilated with horror at the mere thought.

At this instant, small Samuel came running into the kitchen from the porch, with Melinda, as usual, close at his heels.

"Pete Zook's wagon's stoppin' at our place!" he announced.

The news brought the whole family, as one man, to the front porch.

"I seen Pete drivin' to New Holland in this morning," said Aunt Susanna, "and I ast him would he fetch out our mail if they was any, and he sayed yes, he'd ought to do us that for a neighborly favor."

"Here's a express package," Pete announced, calling from his buggy, "and your mail."

Acker went forward to receive them.

"Here's the weekly *New Ery*," Pete went on, doling out the things one at a time; "and a package for Augustus Acker; and a postal card for Elephena."

"I guess the postal card's for 'Gustus, too," called back Elephena. "I don't never get none such."

Pete retained the card in his hand as he looked at her over Augustus' head. "Here is 'Elephena Schwenkfelders' on," he insisted, "so it ain't fur 'Gustus Acker. It's from your mom," he explained; "she says on here how if you don't come on back home before—"

Elephena was at his side in an instant, as she held out her hand for the card. "Gimme here!" she said nervously.

The curiosity of the family as to the postal card made them forget even to thank Pete Zook for his neighborliness. They followed Elephena as she hurried indoors, and gathered about her as in faltering tones she read her mother's communication:

ELEPHENA if yule come back home today before you are got married a'ready to that dopple Aaron Wilt and if yule drop them outlandish Amish Cloes all will be forgave and ile by you a new silk dress right aways and leave you have a party and a trip to Phildelphy. But if you marry that dumn close-fisted feller ile never go to my grave till ive paid you back and him too and all that underhanded soft-soap set of em!

"Now think!" breathed Mrs. Wilt, her mild eyes wide with wonder at such language.

"Ach, such talk!" Levi said, dismissing it summarily by going at once to his place at the table and beginning to help himself. "It ain't sensible, such talk like that there."

"Don't you worry, Elephena," Aaron said manfully. "I won't leave her do you nothing, once we're married. Why, what *kin* she do?"

"She has *somepin'* in her mind fur to do," Elephena said despondently. "When she talks so positive she means somepin'!"

"Well, don't leave her spoil our weddin'-day," coaxed Aaron. "She's made you enough sufferin' a'ready in your life. Now you're *shed* of her!"

"What's your package, 'Gustus? You ain't opened it," Aunt Susanna said, as she moved about the table filling the coffee cups. "Shall I open it for you?"

"Elephena must open it. It is her wedding present from me."

"Well, if I ever!" exclaimed Aunt Susanna.

"Now think!" murmured Naomi.

"I didn't think to get no present off of *you,* 'Gustus!" Elephena cried in childish delight.

"Open and leave us see onct what is it," insisted Aunt Susanna, handing it to Elephena across the table; and everybody stopped eating to watch with bated breath while Elephena obeyed.

It was a tablecloth and a dozen napkins. Acker had thought to do a bit of missionary work in presenting the napkins, inasmuch as his request for one, on the occasion of his first meal at the farm, had led to his being provided with a bureau scarf embroidered in red cotton.

The family seemed overwhelmed with his lavish generosity, and Acker could not be surprised at the fact, in view of the customary ten-cent wedding gifts.

As yet, no presents had arrived for Elephena.

"Will your friends bring their gifts to you when they come tomorrow to the wedding?" he asked as, after his gift had been duly passed round and admired, the family returned to their plates.

"Some, mebbe," Naomi answered him. "One or two or so. But most of 'em not. You see, after they're married, about twict a week they'll go off."

"Go off?" vaguely repeated Acker, unable to think of anything but fireworks.

"Wisitin'," she explained. "On comp'ny. To spend the day at the farms of the different ones where was here at the weddin'. And them different ones will have their present ready till Aaron and Elephena gets there. That's the way us Amish we all do when we get married."

"I wonder," spoke Aunt Susanna as she came to her place at the table, "if Ezra Bushonger's Jennie will be here tomorrow or if she's too far gone to wenture. She's consumpted," she tossed the explanation in a side remark to Acker. "The last I seen her she was wonderful bad."

"I tole Ezra when he begun keepin' comp'ny with her," said Levi, "she didn't look hearty. But he said little women like her was often the heartiest and the best workers. Well, he learnt better!"

"But, Levi," his wife said, "Jennie Bushonger was a wonderful good worker till she got consumpted."

"Yes," declared Aunt Susanna, "as the sayin' is, 'It don't depend on size, or a cow could catch a rabbit.'"

As Aunt Susanna's proverbs were regarded by the family as authoritative as Holy Scripture itself, this quotation settled the matter.

"I'll miss Jennie Bushonger when she's passed away," Aunt Susanna sighed; "she was always so kind to me when we lived neighbors at Elim. Whenever she'd go away on comp'ny to her own folks at Readin', she'd leave me some of her remains—some pies or cold meat or what—where she hadn't used up till she was ready to go. It saved me often from spendin'. And 'If you save in time, you'll have it in need,' as the sayin' is."

After supper, as Sabina was moving about the big kitchen clearing the table, she whispered to Acker in passing, "I got to speak to you a secret—please come on out."

A few minutes later he met her on the front porch.

"Elephena and Aaron they ast me to do 'em somepin' fur a favor," she whispered as they stood close together in the darkness of the autumn evening. "They want me to go over to Elim tonight and ast Elephena's mom or the hired girl fur Elephena's things. But I have afraid to go, her mom's so down on her. She gets so mad sometimes she'll do 'most anything, and I don't know what she might do me. I thought, 'Gustus, if *you'd* mebbe go with—"

She hesitated in some embarrassment, but as Acker said nothing, she went on, "Mebbe

Elephena's mom wouldn't do me nothin' if you was with."

"But why should they send you on such an errand to such a woman?" he asked indignantly. "Your father would not allow you to go if he knew, would he?"

"No. I'll have to go unbeknownst. Aaron he don't like to think of Elephena losin' all them clo'es and things, fur then next winter he'll have to buy some new; so he planned he'd try to get 'em anyways. You see," she explained, "if we wasn't Amish, they could sue fur 'em. But Elephena's mom knows if she won't give 'em up, we can't get 'em, fur us Amish haven't dare to sue."

"I don't believe she'll give them to us, do you?" he asked.

"No, I don't. But, anyways, Aaron and Elephena will feel they done all they could to get 'em."

Acker considered the matter for a moment. "Biney," he finally said, "let me go alone and see what I can do. Maybe I can persuade her to give them up. Surely I'd be more apt to be successful without you. The sight of Aaron's sister would only excite her anger. And I don't think it safe for you to go near the woman."

Sabina demurred a little at this arrangement. It was evident that she longed to be with him.

"I will go alone, Biney. You must stop at home," Acker decided after a pause.

"Leave me go with and wait outside," pleaded Biney.

Acker shook his head. "I would not think of leading you into such danger. I'll go alone and do my best to work the old lady."

CHAPTER TWELVE

ELEPHENA'S "MOM"

IN THE COOL, STIFFLY FURNISHED PARLOR AT
Elim Acker awaited the entrance of the landlady, to whom the "hired girl" had gone to
announce his presence.

As soon as his eyes rested upon the large,
stout woman who presently appeared in the
doorway, he understood her daughter's abject
fear of her. She was of the major-general type
of woman and looked quite able to command
an army. Her eyes were blue and hard. Her face
was so florid that he was sure Aunt Susanna
would have pronounced her case to be chronic
heart disease. She was painfully neat; her hair
was stretched back from her face so tight and
smooth that it hurt one to look at it. Her calico
gown and gingham apron were absolutely
spick-and-span.

"This is Mrs. Schwenkfelders?" Acker asked, rising and bowing as she strode across the room.

"Yes, I'm her. Did you want supper or what? It's some late fur supper; and they was a crowd of pleasure-seekers, or what, come to eat, and it took near all I had. The butter is all. The eggs is run out. And the chickens is run out too."

"But I did not come for dinner."

"Oh, didn't you? Well, then, what d'you want?" A look of suspicion flashed in her eyes. "Say!" Her voice rose shrilly, her florid complexion became apoplectic, and she lowered her head aggressively. "Are you that there boarder the Wilts had last summer?"

Acker was obliged to plead guilty.

"Oh, you are, are you!" she harshly exclaimed. "Well, what did they send you *here* fur, heh? What d'you want?"

Acker saw that his task was not going to be an easy one. He decided to temporize and not at once declare his real errand.

"The Wilt family and your daughter would be very happy if you would attend the wedding tomorrow."

"Attend that there weddin'!" she exclaimed hoarsely, the blood mounting to her hair and spreading over her neck in an appalling manner.

"*Me!* I'd ruther see my daughter dead at my feet than married to that there Amishman! If she wasn't eighteen a'ready, d'you think I'd leave her stay an *hour* in that there house? I'd fetch her home if I had to drag her! *Me* go to that there weddin'! It ain't Elephena where sent you on no *such* dumn urrand! She knows me better'n that!

"Just to think," she mourned, an odd mingling of excitement and plaintiveness in her voice, as she sank into a chair before him, her big arms folded over her ample bosom, "after the way I raised my only child so careful, she'd up and turn Amish unbeknownst to me! And ag'in' my wishes, too! I tole her often all I'd do fur her if she dropped that there Aaron Wilt and married to suit me. But no, she wouldn't listen on me! That's the thanks a mother gets for all she does fur her child yet! But she'll find out somepin' till she's married a couple months!" she predicted, her lips set in a vindictive curve. "She ain't used to livin' so close and countin' every penny, like them Amish do—yes, the richest of 'em! Why look a-here, mister"—she leaned forward, emphasizing her words by pointing her forefinger at him—"them Amish would peel a potato no bigger'n a hickory-nut sooner'n throw it out—that mean they are! Why, that Susanna Wilt, while her man was livin' and she had a-plenty to live on, she'd go to the different Amish farms, still, when they was goin' to butcher a pig, and she'd help all day for the couple pounds of sausage they'd give her, and then, honest to God, if she didn't up and send them sausages to market to *sell!*" Scorn choked her utterance for a moment.

"The Amish are saving, I know," Acker granted when he could get in a word. "But they work so hard for every dollar they earn, no wonder they don't spend it very freely. Aaron will be well off, I understand, and I believe your daughter could not find a husband who would be kinder or gentler to her. And he is a fellow of good principles. You are a woman who knows life well enough to realize how rare such men are and how little his 'closeness' counts against such a consideration."

"D'you think I ain't got no pride?" she angrily demanded. "Not to feel no shame at my daughter's turning Amish and puttin' on them outlandish clo'es? And me I always dressed her so stylish!"

Tears of mingled rage and grief again choked her. But she continued: "And to think she'd be that mean as to up and leave me and join them bigoty people, just when she knowed I needed her help in puttin' up the peaches!"

Acker wondered how he should ever approach the object of his errand.

"And another thing," she continued; "them Amish'll kreistle [disgust] Elephena another way, seein' how clean she's been raised to change her underclo'es once a week. An Amishman he wears his wool shirt on hisself in winter a whole month, and *then* don't have it washed, but only hung out to air while he wears his other one a month. They won't put water to their wool because it shrinks it. But I hold that the air can't make them shirts clean enough without water."

"Nevertheless, Mrs. Schwenkfelders," Acker earnestly expostulated, "hard as it may be to you to have Elephena marry against your wishes, you must recognize that nothing that you can do will prevent it, so why not accept it and make the best of it? I don't blame you for objecting to it, but why beat your head against a stone wall in uselessly opposing them?"

"I tole Elephena what she has to look fur if she marries that there Aaron Wilt!" her mother affirmed with a vindictiveness of look and tone that Acker recognized as hopelessly unconquerable. "I'll never forgive her or speak to her, and she'll not get one dollar off of me as long as she lives, and I'd see her starve first!"

"You are a Lutheran?" Acker quietly asked.

"Yes!" she answered stoutly. "A Lutheran I was raised and a Lutheran I'll always be! And if my own flesh and blood goes back on the religion of her own mother, she needn't look to *me* fur no help—never!"

"Is that the spirit taught in the Lutheran Church? The Amish teach something very different. They seem to believe in charity and forgiveness toward those who despitefully use them."

Mrs. Schwenkfelders seemed at a loss for a reply for an instant. But she quickly rallied her forces. "The Scripture says, 'Children, obey to your parents,' and that's the Scripture *I* go by! And as fur them Amish, if one of *them* marries outside the church they get put off of Meeting and disinherited by their pop."

He saw that further parleying with her would accomplish nothing.

"I came over here, Mrs. Schwenkfelders, to ask you if you will please send Elephena all her little belongings. She wants them sent in her telescope satchel."

"Oh, she does, does she!" Mrs. Schwenkfelders sarcastically exclaimed. "Well, she can keep on wantin'! I'll see myself sendin' her so much as a rag out of this here house!"

"But the clothes are hers," suggested Acker.

"They're hern—them," she defiantly demanded, "when I bought 'em for her with my own money?"

"Elephena surely earned her clothing by the work she did here. Do you think that you have any right to keep her things?"

"Whether I have any right to keep her things?" she furiously repeated, suddenly rising and standing over him in so threatening an attitude that he thought she must intend a personal assault upon him. "Has *she* any right to disobey to my word the way she's did ? Here's what you can tell her and all the rest of 'em, from *me!* That to my dyin' day I'll never rest till I've punished Elephena fur this here act of hern! She'll be made to suffer *some* way, and let her look out! And all them Wilts too! I won't leave no stone unturned to pay 'em back fur takin' my daughter from me! I'll never be satisfied till I have my satisfaction!"

As Acker looked upon her face, distorted with insane anger, he felt that she was undoubtedly capable of the lifelong enmity she declared.

Perceiving that his errand was futile, he gave up the struggle and left her; and she followed him to the door with her vehement reiteration of vengeance-to-come for those who had offended her.

On his homeward walk, he reflected upon how much of life's suffering comes from the evil in one's own heart. "And by far the keener sort of suffering, too. That woman's countenance revealed, beneath all the devil in it, the mother-love at war with her bad passions. Her heart is bleeding at this loss of her child, worse to her than the girl's death could be. And the loss is of her own creation."

Upon his return home, Biney's face of relief betrayed how anxious she had been for his safety. To Elephena the report of his failure was a matter of course. But Aaron's depression, when he was told of it, suggested to Acker that Elephena's future was not to be a bed of roses.

"Poor girl, what unaccustomed petty economies she will have to practise, no matter how prosperous Aaron grows! They are right not to marry 'outside of Meeting.' If they married with those unaccustomed to their frugality, we wouldn't find their homes so peaceful and their countenances so placid."

But in spite of his pity for her, Acker saw that the girl was going to be far happier in her new life than she had ever been with her mother, simply because she would be more free.

"Only people with the natures of dogs are happy in bondage," he thought. "My only real misgiving for the happiness of these two is that melodramatic threat of 'Elephena's mom.' I'm sure she'll carry it out—or die in the attempt."

CHAPTER THIRTEEN

THE MARRIAGE

ACKER WAS UP BETIMES THE NEXT MORNING, not only because he did not wish to hinder the family, but because he was anxious to miss nothing of the curious spectacle of an Amish wedding.

The guests began to arrive at half-past seven, and by half-past eight the stable-yard was filled with Amish wagons, the front parlor stacked with wide-brimmed Amish hats and clumsy hoods of various colors, and the lower floor of the house crowded with men and women, youths and maidens. Acker wondered whether Ulmer would appear.

Aunt Susanna stood at the door to admonish each newcomer not to spoil her clean porch by tracking mud from the damp road across its spotlessness.

"Rub your gums on the grass!" was her repeated admonition before allowing a guest to step on her porch. The first time Acker heard her deliver this order, he was startled; but it appeared that in Aunt Susanna's vocabulary "gums" meant overshoes.

The chairs in the kitchen and other downstairs rooms were arranged as for a Sunday meeting, and Aaron and his bride sat in the front row. The bride wore a black merino gown and shoulder-cape, and a white cap. Acker thought she looked very pretty and demure.

Just before the services began, Ulmer slunk into the kitchen and took a seat near the door, as though, in case his feelings got beyond him, he could easily slip out again. Sabina tried to meet his eye and smile at him from her place across the room. But she was seated near Acker, and Ulmer, after one hasty glance, would not again let his eyes wander in her direction.

Sabina had been very pale all the morning, and Acker had attributed it to the excitement of the occasion. But now, as she sat at his side, he realized that there must be a more serious cause for her pallor. Her eyes, too, wore a haunted, far-seeing expression, and he found his heart contracting with the sharp, sudden fear that she had had another sight of the Face.

"The thing is grotesque!" he told himself, yet his uneasiness remained.

"What's the matter, Biney?" he whispered to her. "You look so white."

"'Gustus!" she whispered back, her voice trembling, "when I fell awake this morning and minded it was Aaron's day to say 'Yes,' I—seen the Face right aways!"

"Have you told anyone, Biney?"

"Only Aaron. He sayed fur me not to speak nothin' to Elephena."

"Try to forget, Biney. Don't believe in it. You may have imagined it this time."

"No." She shook her head. "When I ain't really *seen* it, I can't make out in my thoughts what it looks like wery well. I tried onct or twict; but it ain't never plain to me, unlest it's a warnin'."

Her teeth chattered as she spoke, and only Ulmer's scowling presence prevented his putting his hand on hers to calm her. "Don't let us speak of it, or think of it," he gently urged.

In a short time the preacher took his place in front of the bridal pair, and Acker was doomed to the torment of listening to a three-and-a-half-hours' discourse in Pennsylvania German, not a word of which he understood.

"Biney's vision this morning was certainly a portent of my sufferings under this harangue!" he ruefully thought as he fidgeted in his hard chair.

"What did the preacher find to talk about for more than three mortal hours?" he asked of Sabina, when at last the sermon was over. "What do they preach about at these weddings?"

"They preach a sermon appropriate that way—give good adwices."

"Yes?" he said and awaited further enlightenment.

"Yes," nodded Sabina, conclusively.

The marriage ceremony followed the sermon, and then at half-past twelve the dinner was served. The work was all done, according to time-honored custom at Amish weddings, by the married women present, the "young folks" on a wedding day being exempt from all labor.

"It'll go easy," Aunt Susanna confided to Acker; "there's a good bit of women here to help."

There was not much conversation at the dinner table, everybody being too busy satisfying the demands of hunger following that interminable sermon.

After dinner, the table being cleared and fruit, cake, and pie set out, each unmarried youth chose his girl and sat at her side at the table, with the older people keeping in the background as much as was possible in so crowded a place. The bride and groom occupied the place of honor at one end of the long table.

Acker was invited by Sabina to be her partner, but he begged to be excused. He felt that he would be a restraint upon them. He saw to his regret that his refusal mortified her. She had strained a point to ask him, since it was the maiden's place to be sought, not to seek, for this honor. Unfortunately, just as she was in the act of turning to him to offer him the place at her side, Ulmer Popple, turning to *her* to make the same request, heard her speak to Acker.

The young Amishman's face flushed, then turned pale with anger. He appeared stunned by the fact that Biney should actually think of anyone but him on such a significant occasion.

But the girl did not heed him. She was too much taken up with her evident chagrin in Acker's refusal. Seeing how hurt she was, Acker would undoubtedly have relented and accepted her invitation had he not felt even more sympathy for Ulmer Popple's plight.

"It would make Ulmer too angry," he told Sabina. "We must not spoil the day for him. Ask *him* to sit with you."

Sabina lifted her head proudly. "He can ast me, if he wants. I don't *have* to ast him or any other feller to—well," she faltered, "you're different, because you're a stranger and don't know our ways so different."

Ulmer had promptly selected a pretty Amish girl named Barbara Schnabel, to that damsel's manifest satisfaction, but evidently not to the satisfaction of Levi and Naomi, who looked troubled and annoyed at such a public exhibition as this of the alienation of Sabina and the young man they favored.

It fell to her lot, in this turn of affairs, to sit with an elderly widower who had insisted upon being allowed to join the unmarried "young folks."

The entire company of young people having arranged themselves in couples about the table, the festivities began. Conversation and the singing of hymns alternated with the consumption of large quantities of pie, cake, and fruit. The "conversation" was a strange mixture of Pennsylvania German and corrupt English.

Someone presently proposed "riddles," and the suggestion was enthusiastically taken up. The childlike simplicity of these grown-up young people was quickly manifested in the hilarious amusement they found in their riddles.

"Where does it have the most wet stones? It has in the water the most wet stones."

"Where was the first nail knocked at? On its head."

"What has its heart in its head? Cabbage."

"What comes after cheese? Mice."

"How far does the crow fly in the woods? Till the middle; then it flies out again."

"Before what does the fox run up the mountain? Before his tail."

This riddle seemed to strike Biney's partner, the widower, as excruciatingly funny. "That's a choke!" he cried, shaking with laughter. "A choke!" he repeated, slapping the table.

But Ulmer Popple, it appeared, did not catch the point. "What fur choke is that?" he sullenly asked. "*I* don't see no choke."

"Why, don't you see—the fox runs up the mountain before what? Before his tail! His tail it comes after him." The widower leaned back and roared with laughter, and everyone but Ulmer and Sabina joined him.

"Now, Ulmer, it's your turn to give one," Barbara Schnabel reminded him with a poke of her elbow.

"Why does a rooster step over a wheel-rut?" Ulmer asked in an uninterested tone. He was evidently not enjoying himself.

Sabina was familiar with all the riddles and other mental furniture in Ulmer's possession, and she promptly gave the answer. "It is too far to walk round."

They kept this up until suppertime. Later, a succession of childish games was played with all the zest of young children. It ended in a wild romp in the barn, even sober Sabina and chagrined Ulmer catching the spirit of the time. This romp was prolonged until midnight, and during the final outburst of hilarity they carried out the custom of throwing the bridegroom over the fence to indicate that he no longer belonged to the "young folks."

Acker did not stay up to see the end of it all. At eleven o'clock he went to bed exhausted, feeling, now that Elephena and Aaron were safely married and there had been no interference from the girl's mother, no tragedy would come to the newly wedded pair that night, at least. He speculated, before he slept, as to whether Ulmer and Sabina would "make up" before parting for the night.

Just before dozing off, he heard the bride and groom enter the room prepared for them next to his own. They had probably never heard of "the world's custom" of a wedding journey.

CHAPTER FOURTEEN

SABINA HAS A PREMONITION

THE NEXT MORNING ACKER, AGAINST HIS OWN natural inclinations, pleaded that his duties in town obliged him to return at once, and so prevented his waiting until Monday morning to accompany Sabina. Upon this Sabina promptly suggested that she leave a day earlier in order to have company on the trip. But her father would not allow her to travel in the trolley cars on Sunday, and there was no appeal from his quietly delivered command.

Acker now set himself to avoid any communication with the girl, and for two months he succeeded in holding to his resolution. He was inclined to believe that she would soon weary in her attendance at the Normal School.

As the days went on and he received no word from her, he began to feel sure that she had already returned to the farm. He told himself that he hoped soon to receive an invitation to another Amish wedding.

Meantime, he often wondered how Mrs. Schwenkfelders was going to make good her threats. An uneasiness for the safety of Aaron and Elephena he found obtruding itself upon his attention very often.

In a singular way these Amish acquaintances, with whom he had nothing in common, had most securely intrenched themselves in his life and thoughts, and he continued to take a lively interest in their small affairs.

One evening, as he was sitting in his room, working hard on a sketch of Biney as he had first seen her in her purple sunbonnet, he was suddenly summoned to the telephone.

With a sigh of boredom at the interruption, he dropped his pencil and went downstairs to answer the summons.

"Hello!"

"This is Mr. Acker?" said a sweet feminine voice over the wires—a familiar voice which he could not instantly recall.

"Yes," he answered.

"This is the office of the Normal School."

"Oh, yes, and this is the secretary?"

"Yes. Miss Wilt is in great distress and insists, against the wishes of the preceptress, upon going out to New Holland tonight. She is about to start now and asks you to meet her at the square and put her on the New Holland car."

"I shall be there—tell her, please," he promptly answered. "Is she ill?"

"No. Unless—it seems to be some mental trouble. She thinks she's had a presentiment of trouble at home—she has had no message, but she is convinced that someone at her home is in distress and she must go home at once. The preceptress thinks that she is beside herself with homesickness. She can't possibly get to New Holland before eleven o'clock, and then she has two miles to ride—or walk."

"I will go with her all the way to her home."

"Will you? Well—"

"I shall see her to her father's home, and then wire or write you immediately of her safety," he reassuringly repeated.

"Well. Thank you."

She rang him off, and he hurried back to his room at once, to throw a few things into a hand-satchel and change his coat. Telling his landlady that he would not be back until the next day, he went out to the square to meet the half-past-nine car from Millersville.

He speculated, while he waited in the brilliantly lighted square, as to whether the

preceptress was right in thinking Sabina's presentiment only an unconquerable attack of
homesickness, or whether the girl actually had
seen that Face again. And if she had, would it
once more prove itself an omen of evil?

The minutes seemed hours while he waited.
His mind was tense with curiosity and with an
anxiety, which he could not reason away.

The moment he saw Sabina, as she got off
the car, he knew that the spell of the Face was
upon her; for her cheeks were pallid and her
eyes dilated with the horror they always wore in
this condition.

She did not speak as he shook hands with her
and led her over to the New Holland car, which
stood waiting at the other side of the square. Her
gaze seemed to look through and past him with
the uncanny effect of clairvoyance that he now
knew so well.

It was not until they were well on their way
that he was able to elicit any coherent account
from the agitated girl.

Yes, she had seen the Face—quite suddenly, as usual, when she had not been
thinking at all of anything gruesome or
unpleasant. One of the scholars—a young
man—had met and walked with her in the
grounds just before supper, and while she was

speaking with him, like a flash, the Face had
come before her mental vision clear and dis-
tinct. She had shuddered and felt as though
she were going to faint, and the alarmed
young man had led her into the house and
summoned the preceptress.

They had refused her permission to go home
that night and had insisted that she must wait
until morning; but she had told them she was
going, that nothing could prevent her; and she
had forced them to let her go.

"Sabina, describe this face to me—can you?
Tell me as nearly as possible what it looks like,"
he urged her.

"It has red hair and whiskers and a cut
upper lip. Its eyes are wery small and set close
side by each. It's all smallpox-marked and it's
wonderful ugly."

"Is that all?"

"That's all I mind of."

"And you can't recall ever having seen such a
person in life?"

"I don't mind of it."

They rode a long distance without talking,
each absorbed in the apprehension of what
might meet them at their journey's end.
Acker saw that, while it was vaguely comfort-
ing to Sabina to have him with her, she was

far too worried and fearful to show pleasure in his presence.

At New Holland, in spite of the lateness of the hour, he was able to hire a buggy, and they drove rapidly out to the farm.

As they neared the end of their drive, he found his heart beating fast with a growing dread.

When at last they drew up at the gate of the Wilt farmhouse, no sign of any trouble or disaster was evident; the house was dark and silent, as was naturally to be expected at eleven o'clock at night. Evidently everyone was abed and asleep. Was Sabina's warning going to prove false this time? While Acker tied the horse, the girl ran up the board walk and knocked loudly on the front door. He joined her on the porch immediately, and they waited a minute for an answer to their summons. But none came. They knocked again and again. There was no response. Sabina shuddered, and Acker felt himself grow cold.

"Pop ain't no heavy sleeper that way. And him and mom sleeps downstairs, too!" Sabina whispered. "Aunt Susanna she falls awake if a *mouse* walks acrost the floor!"

"They're away from home. That's all."

"They don't never *all* go off and leave the house, except on Sundays, still."

"Look!"

Acker had stepped to the edge of the porch, and in the distance, across a wide expanse of fields, he caught a glimpse of a lighted house. No country house would be lighted up, he knew, at this time of night, unless there was either illness in the household or some festivity going on.

"It's Aaron's home!" breathed Sabina as she followed his gaze, "Lights up stairs and down!"

"They're all over there!" Acker said with conviction.

In a moment he and Sabina were in the buggy again and speeding down the road to the neighboring farm.

It was Aunt Susanna who opened the door as their buggy drew up to the gate. She stood on the threshold and held the lamp high to light their path to the house.

"Biney! Is it *you!*" She almost dropped the lamp in her startled surprise. "I thought it was Elephena's mom when I heard the buggy. Oh, Biney, did that Face give you warnin' again?"

The woman was pale and worn, and her eyes were red and swollen.

"Yes! What is it—tell me!" Sabina grasped her aunt's arm as she stood before her on the porch.

"Come in first and set. Oh, 'Gustus!"

She snatched her apron to her eyes and gulped down a sob as she gave him her hand. "To think what's happened us! And you brang Biney home, ain't? I knowed the minute I seen her that she must of had that warnin' again, for she couldn't of got Levi's message a'ready— not till tomorrow mornin'. He wrote her a postal card."

They entered the front best room, and Aunt Susanna placed the lamp on the table. A death-like stillness hung over the house; not a sound came to them. But an inner room, opening from the one in which they stood, was lighted, and the door was ajar.

"Set," urged Aunt Susanna in a whisper, pushing two chairs toward them.

"*Tell* me, Aunt Susanna!" cried Sabina, moving past the chairs and again grasping her aunt's arm. "What's happened? Is Aaron kilt?"

"It ain't Aaron," said Aunt Susanna, tearfully. "It's the bride-elect." Acker had so referred to Elephena on the eve of her marriage, and the epithet appealed to her so irresistibly that she had reveled in using it ever since. "The bride-elect she's with the angels."

Acker felt the room suddenly swirl before his eyes. He steadied himself to hear Sabina gasp, "Did—did her mom kill her?"

"No, no! Her mom ain't know nothin' till we sent and tole her. And we're lookin' fur her over. We can't think she won't come. But she ain't here yet, and it was six o'clock when we sent word for—"

"How did Elephena die?"

Sabina sank into the chair now and pressed her white face against the tidy which hung over the back of it; and Aunt Susanna sat down before them both.

"She got thinner and sparer every day and so wonderful weak! She was to have her baby till spring a'ready. . . . Well, this after, at four o'clock, when Aaron he come from the barn in, to see, onct, was supper ready, here was Elephena layin' in the kitchen in a swoond. Aaron he sent the hired man fur the doctor, and Aaron he done what he could himself to bring her to, but till the doctor got there at five o'clock, he sayed she was dead. He sayed it was her heart stopped beatin' from weakness."

"At five o'clock the doctor sayed she was dead?" Sabina leaned forward in her chair, her eyes fixed on her aunt's, as she asked the question.

"Yes. Was it—was it then, Biney, that that there Face come before you?" quavered Aunt Susanna.

"It was just before supper, and we eat at half-past five!"

"Now look at that!" whispered Aunt Susanna, turning a horrified glance at Acker. "Ain't it wonderful queer? Your pop wouldn't of had need to waste that there postal card!"

"Is everybody here—mom and all?" Sabina asked without opening her eyes.

"Yes. Aaron's in there," she whispered, twisting her thumb toward the inner room, "with the corp'. The rest's up in bed. The undertaker was here till nine o'clock."

"How's poor Aaron?" Acker asked in a low voice.

"He acts like he had fell off the barn on his head!" Aunt Susanna answered, a sob in her voice. "He ain't hardly spoke since. He just sets and stares. He thought so wonderful much of Elephena—poor Aaron!"

"Do any of you suspect foul play? Do you suspect Elephena's mother of having injured her?"

"Beware!" Aunt Susanna quickly warned him. "That's much said, 'Gustus!"

"Trust me to be cautious. But *have* you any suspicion?"

"We don't know no more'n what I tole you. As the sayin' is, 'What we know not burns us not!'"

"What sort of a doctor have you had?"

"We had Dr. Hess from New Holland over."

"A regular physician? Not a quack?"

"He's graduated and got such a diarploma—what you call it? Hangin' in his office up."

The stair door opened softly, and Mrs. Wilt appeared on the steps that came down into the front room. Her dress was thrown on loosely, and she held it together with a nervous hand. Her braids of hair hung down her back, and she wore no cap. Evidently she had just got out of bed. In spite of the heavy trouble in her countenance, Acker was struck with the youthfulness of her appearance in the absence of her prim cap.

She came to Sabina, and mother and daughter kissed without speaking. As Acker rose and took her hand, she raised her Madonna face to his, and her brimming eyes expressed her motherly gratitude to him for his care of Sabina in bringing her home.

"Come up and see pop, Biney," she whispered to the girl.

"Sha'n't I go in there"—Sabina pointed to the room where Aaron kept vigil—"and speak to Aaron?"

"Wait till the morning. He ain't rightly at himself tonight, poor boy!" the mother's voice of deep pity answered her, and they left the room together.

Acker sat up a while longer, listening to the details of poor Elephena's symptoms during the past few months, which Aunt Susanna, he foresaw, would never tire of relating.

"Well," she concluded with a long sigh, "it's plain Elephena's mom ain't comin' over *tonight*, anyhow. You'd think she'd of come as soon as she otherwise could, after she'd heard it; ain't? How *kin* any person hold spite ag'in' her own offspring where's passed away?" she said wonderingly. "To think that mebbe she won't be at her own daughter's funeral! It does, now, beat all, the feelin's some folks can cherish that's in the world!"

Acker rose at length to suggest that he would now either drive on to the nearest hotel or, if he could be accommodated here, go out and put up his horse for the night.

She assured him it would be a comfort to all to have him with them; and as neither Aunt Susanna nor any other member of the family was given to making complimentary speeches or saying what was not meant, he consented to stay.

CHAPTER FIFTEEN

MRS. SCHWENKFELDERS

SABINA'S PREMONITION DID NOT, AT THIS TIME, impress the family as deeply as usual, because, under the tragic circumstances which quickly followed, there was neither time nor emotion to spare for any lesser experience.

The next morning found Aaron still in the same dazed state in which he had been ever since the doctor's fatal words had fallen on his ears. And he continued to stare out of hollow, vacant eyes upon all his little world. Mechanically he followed his father to the barn and helped him with the necessary chores about the place. Dumbly he sat at the breakfast table with the family and ate his tasteless food. Deep emotions or strong passions were not characteristic of the Amish, and even the mild, steadfast domestic affections, which were, as a rule, their strongest feelings, found scant external expression with them. Aaron's stunned, wordless grief was like the hurt of a wounded animal.

His morning's tasks finished, he resumed his vigil of the night before, shutting himself up alone with his dead bride.

Acker was impressed with the tenderness of Biney's nature as it stood revealed in her evident suffering for Aaron. Her quiet ministrations to him, the look of pain in her eyes, the melting softness of her tones, showed a heart of gentleness and love that touched him deeply.

It was in the midst of their vast cooking preparations for the funeral, at which a meal must be served to all the Amish of the country-side, that the family were startled by the sudden and violent arrival of Elephena's mother, Mrs. Schwenkfelders. She swooped down upon this house of mourning like an all-conquering army upon a defenseless foe.

At sound of the buggy wheels at the gate, the whole family, save Aaron, gathered in the front room to meet her; their uncertainty as to the greeting she would give them, and their timidity before a nature so foreign to their own phlegmatic temperament, were manifested painfully in the shrinking aspect of all.

Levi opened the door for her as she came up the board walk.

"Where is my daughter? Leave me go to her!" she demanded, striding in among the stricken family as they stood grouped about the room. The woman's face was livid with conflicting emotions—grief for this sudden, untimely death of her only child, warring with her hot hatred of those who, she felt, had brought it about.

Melinda and Sammy drew away from her in terror and clung whimpering to Sabina's skirts.

"Wait till I call Aaron away; then I'll leave you go in to It," Levi said to her in lowered tones. "Aaron's settin' with It."

"Where is she? Where is my child?" the woman almost shrieked in her frenzy of sorrow and hate. "I'm not waitin' fur Aaron nor no one! Take me to my poor daughter! Why didn't you leave me *know* she was sick and dyin', so I could come to her!" she cried out as though from a bursting heart. "Here you kep' it to yourselfs, and I knew nothin' till this morning, when I come from East Donegal over and am told at the store yet! Is *that* your Amish religion where you uphold to and—"

"We sent you word over last evening as soon as it happened," spoke Levi, calmly. "If you was away, that's why you didn't get our message."

She turned her flashing, swollen eyes upon him. "Oh, you did send me word, did you? Yes, till she was dead a'ready! Why wasn't I left know she was ailin'? Me, her own mother!"

"We didn't know what it would give till she died fur us—it was that sudden and unexpected," Levi replied, his voice growing more quiet as hers became more uncontrolled.

"Yes, I guess!" she bitterly retorted. "You're a set o' smooth-tongued hypocrites! You kep' it from me to spite me—that's what you done! Leave me go to her! Where is she?"

"Wait here a minute."

Levi turned to the inner chamber, but she strode after him, reiterating that she wasn't waiting "fur no one." He turned before the closed door and barred her way. "You can't come in here till I tell Aaron to come out. You tried to hurt him onct; you can't have no second chanct if I can help."

The woman was nearly a head taller than Levi and of far more powerful build. In her inflamed state of mind she would not brook his opposition for an instant; lifting her great arms, she pushed him aside as though he were a child. But before she could lay her hand on the knob of the door, Mrs. Wilt and Acker were at her side to prevent her.

"Don't leave her in there to Aaron!" cried Naomi, feebly. "She'll do him somepin'! Levi! 'Gustus! Don't leave her in!"

"You must wait until we can ask Aaron to come out, Mrs. Schwenkfelders," Acker commanded, wedging himself between the huge woman and the door to guard it. "Move back, please, while Levi goes in for a moment."

"Who are *you* to be keepin' me from my own—"

"Here, Levi!"

Acker flung open the door, then forced the woman back to allow him to enter.

"How darst you!" she furiously cried. "Take your hands off of me, or—"

"Mrs. Schwenkfelders, you forget this is a house of mourning. We must insist that you be quiet."

The man's firm voice subdued her for the moment. She glared at him like an animal at bay, while Levi slipped into the room and locked the door after him.

"Yous are *afraid* to leave me in to her—yous are hidin' somepin' from me!"

Acker saw that the woman was almost beside herself and hardly knew what she said.

"You shall go in in a moment, Mrs. Schwenkfelders," he repeated in his controlling voice.

Even as he spoke, the door opened, and Aaron and his father came forth. Aaron's dazed eyes seemed scarcely to see his mother-in-law as he walked past her and went outdoors. The look of fierce hatred which she cast upon him he did not notice.

She rushed upon the open door, disappeared behind it, and the frightened family heard the key turn in the lock.

The outraged and unforgiving mother was alone with her dead daughter.

She remained shut in the room for nearly an hour. They could hear her loud weeping, now and then, as they went about their work. That her grief was sincere none of them for a moment doubted. Her anguished face gave sufficient testimony to that. She was a woman of violent passions, whether of love or of hate, and her rage at her daughter's marriage had only been commensurate with her disappointed ambitions for the child she had borne and reared in self-sacrifice and devotion—a devotion often tyrannical and misguided and marred by her uncontrollable temper at the least contradiction of her will, but a devotion, nevertheless, that would have given her very life for what *she* regarded as her daughter's welfare.

Just before her arrival at the farm, Acker had been about to return to Lancaster. But he felt that while this dangerous woman was in the house, he must not go away. Naomi and Aunt Susanna confirmed him in this opinion by their protesting against his leaving—not to mention Sabina's pleading eyes. They felt that it needed the combined strength of both him and Levi to protect the family from "Elephena's mom."

"Could you stay with us until after the funeral?" Naomi timidly urged. "We'd take it wonderful kind if you'll do us that for a favor."

He could ill spare the time, but he saw that his duty lay here. So he said he would remain.

Aaron's hired man was sent to New Holland with the horse and buggy, and Acker went on guard, as it were, in the front room, to wait until Mrs. Schwenkfelders should come forth.

There was nothing in the house for him to read but the weekly *New Era* and the Bible. So he put in his time on the Book of Job, with frequent interruptions from Sabina, who made many obviously useless errands into the room.

It was well to have fortified himself, before he was called upon to meet the difficult circumstances which the rest of that day brought forth, with some of the high philosophy of the patient Job.

The loud weeping in the inner room had been hushed for some time, and no sound whatever had come to him where he sat, a few feet from the door; when suddenly, without warning, the door was jerked open, and Mrs. Schwenkfelders, her face crimson, her eyes bulging and bloodshot, rushed upon him.

"Where's that there Aaron?" she hoarsely demanded, grasping Acker's arm in a clutch that made him wince. "Where's he at?"

She held a bottle in her hand containing a white powder. Acker saw that it was labeled "Arsenic."

"What do you want? What is the matter?" he asked in an authoritative voice.

Sabina, her mother, and Aunt Susanna appeared in the doorway opening to the kitchen, their faces pale with apprehension.

"This here's what I found on the mantel in there!" shrilly cried the woman. "A bottle of *arsenic* yet! My daughter's been murdered! Murdered by her own husband or by his folks! *That's* why she went off that suddent! She was gave this here arsenic! It's like these dumn Amish to let the bottle out where anyone could see it, and not to have knew enough to cover up their own tracks! Yes! My daughter's been murdered! I always *sayed* I'd pay back Aaron Wilt fur takin'

her from me, and now I'll have him hanged by
the law! That's what I'll—"

"You brought that arsenic here yourself,"
Acker calmly affirmed, jumping to the conclusion that this accusation of murder was the
form which the woman's threatened vengeance
was taking.

"Oh," she mockingly cried, "so you're in with
'em, to defend 'em in their crime! I'll have you
arrested along with the rest of them! I'll—"

Sabina darted forward and stood in front of
Acker as if to protect him; but he gently put her
aside and held her hand.

"Was that bottle of arsenic on the mantel
before Mrs. Schwenkfelders went into the
room?" He turned to the frightened Naomi
and put the question.

"Yes. I seen it on the mantel settin'. I didn't
know right what it was."

Mrs. Schwenkfelders laughed shrilly. "She's
too dumn to try to save her own son from hangin'! Yous all heerd her what she sayed, that
there bottle *was* there before I went in!"

She strode past them all and went to the
door. "I'm sendin' over the New Holland coroner till before noon a'ready! *He'll* know if my
child's been gave arsenic or not by her own

husband. And if she has, Aaron Wilt'll be in jail when the funeral is, instead of chief mourner!"

She jerked open the front door and went out, not closing it behind her. Acker dropped Sabina's hand and went across the room to close it, then turned to the trembling women.

"You need not be alarmed," he tried to reassure them. "She can't do any harm. Let her send the coroner if she wants to, and let him hold his inquest." He hesitated an instant, then came nearer to them. "But there is one thing"—he spoke in a lowered voice—"tell me—could it be possible that Elephena was despondent and perhaps took her own life with arsenic? In that case, if the coroner finds arsenic in the stomach—I don't want to alarm you, but we must be prepared and armed against such a woman as Mrs. Schwenkfelders in her present state of mind."

"I never took notice to her bein' downhearted much," Naomi answered. "She was wonderful glad she was goin' to have her baby, fur all she had so weak and sick."

"Then you are sure it was not suicide? Of course," he hastily added, "I am not suspecting that it was. I only want you to be prepared for Mrs. Schwenkfelders and the coroner."

"I'm as sure it wasn't suicide as I am that *I* wouldn't do no such a thing like take a dose of poison," Mrs. Wilt affirmed.

"Then we needn't apprehend anything serious from the inquest, and Mrs. Schwenk-felders will be powerless to do you any injury," he assured them.

When they had returned to the kitchen and he was alone, he slowly and thoughtfully paced the room, his hands clasped behind him. What was the meaning of that bottle of arsenic on the mantel?

There was probably not a case on record of a member of the Amish sect being tried in the courts for any least misdemeanor whatever; and that so quiet and inoffensive a family as the Wilts should be shaken to its foundations by a trial for murder seemed unthinkable. Even Ulmer's persistent devotion would be put to the test by such a disgrace as that.

CHAPTER SIXTEEN

THE INQUEST

IN THE COURSE OF THE MORNING THE CORONER with his six jurymen and the doctor arrived at the farm.

Acker found himself more nervously anxious than the circumstances seemed to warrant, while in the outer room he waited, with the dazed family, to hear what the verdict would be. Surely there could be no ground for apprehending that it would be disastrous to Aaron in any sense. And yet Mrs. Schwenkfelders was almost capable, he verily believed, of bribing a coroner to involve her son-in-law in trouble. Still, it was not likely that the New Holland coroner would chance to be a person capable of the crime of a false testimony which would endanger the life of another, or that he would be able to corrupt his jury and physician.

"I ast Aaron about the arsenic bottle," Sabina whispered to him as she came and sat on the settee at his side.

He turned to her eagerly. Her pallor lent a refinement to her face that made it more than pretty—it was beautiful.

"What did he tell you, Biney?"

"He says a horse-dealer tole him if he gev a dose of arsenic to a horse he was a-goin' to sell, it would make the horse look so sleek and shiny and fat that it would fetch more. That's what Aaron he bought the arsenic fur—to give to his horse to make him fetch more when he solt him."

"The simplicity of his duplicity!" Acker smiled to himself. "It will surely all come right, Biney," he reassured her.

But when the coroner, with the jurymen and the doctor, came forth at last from the chamber of death, the sight of their faces made Acker's heart contract. What had they found?

The coroner's shocked glance swept the faces of the family uncertainly, almost shrinkingly, and he avoided looking at Aaron. The stricken widower, however, seemed less concerned than any other member of the family as to what he might have to say.

The coroner picked up his overcoat from the settee, drawing it on as he came across the room, and stopped at Acker's chair.

"Mister," he said, bending and speaking in a low voice, "will you give me dare to speak somepin' to you out on the front porch?"

Acker left Sabina's side and silently followed him and his men out of doors.

"Say, mister," the man began apologetically, as soon as the door was closed behind them, "I got to do my dooty, fur all I'm that wonderful sorry to bring trouble to such a old family of our neighborhood as these here Wilts. They always lived respectable. And to have such trouble and disgrace like what this here is comin' on 'em—it don't go easy with me to be the informant ag'in' 'em. I want to ast you to do me this fur a favor, that you'll break it to 'em that I'll have to inform the aw-thorities about this here arsenic in the stomeek of the corp', and that Aaron will likely have to be arrested."

"What!" demanded Acker. "You say you found arsenic in the stomach?"

"That's what. We're takin' the stomeek with, to use it fur evidence. I got to do my dooty. I ain't got no choice."

"You are going to have that poor fellow arrested?" Acker indignantly questioned. "You know he never gave her poison! And if she had any arsenic she took it herself by mistake. Don't, for God's sake, make the blunder of getting this family into such difficulty needlessly! It is preposterous to attach any suspicion to Aaron."

"I only got to do what the law requires off of me," the coroner returned. "I got the stomeek along. I'm takin' it to a chemist that's spendin' the winter in at New Holland; so I ain't got to go in to Lancaster with it. If this here chemist says the same as what Doc Hess, here, says, then Aaron he'll be arrested; for I got to lay the case before the aw-thorities and leave them do what they want. It's easy seen *what* they'll do in a case like this here. I can't hold back what I know."

Before Acker could reply to this, the front door opened and Levi came out.

"What's the matter?" he asked with a resolution to be answered that could not be gainsaid.

Acker repeated to him the coroner's statement that arsenic had been found in the dead woman's stomach. "But," he hastened to add, "as I have told the coroner, Elephena must have taken it herself. No suspicion can attach itself to Aaron."

"All the same," repeated the coroner, "I got to tell you, Levi Wilt, what I tole mister here—I got to leave the chemist examine the stomeek and then lay the fac's before the aw-thorities. I ain't got no choice not to."

"What will the aw-thorities do?" Levi asked in a steady voice; but his hand shook as he put it on Acker's shoulder to steady himself.

"I'm afraid they'll think they got to put the suspicioned party under arrest," the coroner reluctantly conceded. "I'm wonderful sorry, Levi, and I hope you won't lay it up ag'in' *me*. I'm only dischargin' my dooty."

Levi leaned heavily against the house. He could not speak.

"See here, coroner!" Acker turned to the officer abruptly. "I am a graduate of Cornell—scientific course—and hold my degree of Doctor of Science. Let me go with you to your chemist and be present at the examination; and let me add my testimony to his. Will you?"

"Sure, if you want. It don't make *me* no difference. If you're a doctor of sciences you ought to know arsenic when you see it."

"There ain't no doubt in *my* mind," put in the village doctor, who had joined them, "that Elephena Wilt she died of an overdose of arsenic, whether she took it herself or *whatever*."

Acker went indoors and got his coat and hat.

"I'll come back as soon as I can and relieve your suspense," he told Levi. "Meantime, don't distress your family with this suspicion. It isn't necessary. The thing *can't* come to any trial; it's too absurd. I'll do what I can to straighten it out for you all."

Levi looked at him gratefully; but no words came to his colorless lips.

Acker and the coroner got into the latter's buggy, and together they drove away.

All the way to town Acker felt sick at heart as he thought of the effect of this day of horror upon the sensitive soul of Biney.

It was not until nine o'clock that night that Acker returned to the farm. All the family, save Levi, had gone to bed. The father, who alone knew of the danger which threatened his son, had been unable to go to sleep and was sitting up to let Acker in when he should come back.

"I'd begun to conceit you wasn't comin' back no more tonight," Levi whispered, as, after bolting and locking the front door, the two men came across the room and sat down at a center-table on which a kerosene lamp burned low. "I was gettin' so onrestless I had half a mind to hitch up and drive in to see what was keepin' you so. Anyways, they ain't been out yet to arrest

Aaron," he said huskily. "What are you got to report, 'Gustus?"

He asked the question falteringly, for Acker's face was not reassuring. Its pallor, exhaustion, and anxiety portended the worst.

"At first I thought the coroner had perhaps been bribed by Mrs. Schwenkfelders," he began; but Levi shook his head.

"No; he's as honest as a coroner otherwise could be. To be sure, it's a government job, bein' a coroner is, and all governments is corrupt and of the devil. But Jake Eby he wouldn't leave Elephena's mom bribe him to get Aaron in no such trouble. I knowed him this long time back a'ready, and he ain't that kind of man. If he sayed they found arsenic in Elephena's stomeek, then they *found* it. The bother is how did it get there?"

"Well, the chemist and I together made the analysis, and we found an enormous quantity of arsenic. But the large quantity was proof positive that it had never been *swallowed*—for, as I pointed out to the other fellow, it is a physical impossibility to retain such an amount of arsenic for a minute; it would instantly be vomited. A small dose may be retained and be fatal. A large dose can't be. We found ten times the normal dose. How did it get there? While we puzzled over the matter, the constable came in. Mrs. Schwenkfelders had sent him to learn the result of the inquest. He insisted that all *he* wanted to know was that both of us had found arsenic in the stomach of the deceased. This, with the damning testimony of the bottle on the mantel, was enough to warrant the arrest of the husband. How the arsenic got into the stomach was none of *our* business, he said. The courts would investigate that. We had done our part in proving that *it was there.* He would subpœna us both as witnesses in due time. He would not listen to my affirmation that such a quantity of arsenic as that we had found could not possibly have been swallowed."

"Will they leave Aaron be till the funeral's over, d'you think?" Levi asked.

"I'm afraid they won't give him even that respite. No doubt he will be taken away early tomorrow morning. I tell you, Levi, so that you may prepare him and his mother and Sabina. It is dreadful, dreadful for you all. I tried hard to avert it."

Levi put out his hand and clasped Acker's. "You done noble, 'Gustus. I seen, while you was talkin' to me just now, what I never seen before, that education can be put to *use* sometimes. It would of come in handy in this here trouble, only fur that there constable's bein' too dumn or too stubborn-headed to see into them points where your learnin' ferreted out. But"—his voice broke—"it'll 'most kill Aaron to be dragged away before the funeral is."

Acker plunged his hand into his hair and leaned his elbow on the table. "It's all horrible!" he said.

"Will Aaron have to stay in jail till his trial is?"

"If they arrest him, yes. I'm still hoping to think up a way to avoid the arrest."

"I don't see how you kin. But in the trial, 'Gustus, you'll do what you kin, I know, to save my son, won't you?"

Acker, in his turn, leaned forward and clasped Levi's hard old hand in his.

"Nothing that I can do shall be left undone," he said heartily.

"How can you hope fur to awert the arrest?" Levi asked. "I don't see how you kin."

"I don't, either, now. But something may occur to me in the night. That arsenic got into the stomach *somehow.* The question is, *how?* If I can solve that, I can avert the arrest."

"Would they listen at you, any more'n that constable listened at you about the stomeek not holdin' more'n just so much arsenic?"

"If I had *proof.*"

He rose with a deep breath and walked back and forth a few times across the room. After a moment he paused again by the table. "Let us go to bed and try to rest, Levi. I suppose we sha'n't be able to, but we shall have to try. Tomorrow will demand all our strength."

"It ain't no wonder, is it," Levi observed as he picked up the lamp with unsteady hand, "that Biney seen that Face ag'in before all *this* happened us?"

Acker reached forward and relieved him of the lamp. "I'm a little steadier than you are. Better let me carry it."

They went upstairs to spend a sleepless night—Acker to wrestle with the mystery as to how that arsenic had got into the stomach of the dead woman; and Levi to turn over in his mind, in every imaginable form, how he would break it to Naomi, Sabina, and Aaron, in the morning, that an arrest and trial for murder were impending.

CHAPTER SEVENTEEN

ACKER SOLVES A MYSTERY

ACKER WOULD HAVE GIVEN A DOLLAR FOR A CUP of strong coffee to steady his nerves next morning at the five-o'clock breakfast which he took with the family; but it was not to be had, and he was obliged to drink cold skimmed milk instead. He realized, as the family gathered in silence about the table, that they all knew of the danger which threatened the stricken Aaron.

No one could eat much breakfast, and very soon they had all dispersed to their tasks. Biney remained in the kitchen to clear off the table, and Acker, too restless to settle to anything, stayed with her, pacing the floor because he was too nervous to sit still.

"'Gustus!" said the girl, suddenly, as she paused in her work.

"What, Sabina?"

"I was just thinkin' what'll I feel *next* time I see that there Face again! After its warnin' me of all this *here* trouble, why, if I ever see it again I'll go crazy!"

"For God's sake, Sabina, try to forget it."

"It wouldn't stay away fur my *tryin'* not to see it. It always has came to me suddint that way, without my thinkin' about it. And if ever I do see it again—oh, 'Gustus, I'd ruther die than see it again!"

"No wonder, poor child!" he said compassionately, coming and standing at her side. "But don't keep dreading it, for I'm convinced that's the surest way to make it return to you."

"If I see it again," she repeated, her eyes wide with distress, "I'll take it to mean our Aaron's goin' to be hung fur murder!"

She shuddered from head to foot, and Acker quickly laid his cool, firm hand on hers to steady her.

He might have succeeded, but the sound just then of approaching carriage wheels gave the girl's overwrought nerves a new shock. "Is it—is it the policemen?" she gasped, clutching Acker's hand convulsively.

"No, no," he reassured her as he glanced out of the window. "It's some of the funeral guests, I suppose. See!"

Two buggies and a double carriage had drawn up to the gate, and eight Amish-clad figures were alighting; one was Ulmer Popple.

"Yes." She drew a long breath of relief. "They come early on us, ain't? And the funeral don't take up till one o'clock yet. But every time I hear wheels this mornin' I'll conceit it's the police if it ain't the undertaker."

Acker turned from the window abruptly and faced her, a sudden excitement in his eyes.

"*The undertaker!* Ah!"

Sabina stared at him questioningly. "What ails you, 'Gustus?"

"The undertaker! Of course! Why did I never think of that? What an ass! Sabina! Where's Aaron?"

Sabina pointed a thumb in the direction of the inner room.

"Send your father here instantly!" he commanded, in a low voice. "Don't lose a minute, Sabina, if you would save Aaron from jail!"

The girl darted away, and Acker hurried to the door of the death-chamber. He knocked and turned the knob, but it was locked. There was no response from within.

"Aaron!" he called desperately, shaking the door with irreverent loudness.

He heard a heavy step come slowly across the room, and then the key was turned, and Aaron's white gaunt face confronted him.

"Come out, Aaron. I want to speak with you!" he whispered, drawing the young man out and closing the door behind him.

"Are they here fur me—the police?"

"No; and you and I must go to town as fast as your mare can take us, to the undertaker's! I've thought of something which must avert your arrest. Don't stop to ask me what! Get into your coat and come! Levi!" He turned to the father, who had arrived at Sabina's summons. "Hitch the mare to the buggy—or, no! Ask one of those Amishmen out there to let us have *his* buggy immediately to get to town—Aaron and I. We must not lose an instant; we must get to the undertaker's before the policemen get out here, or it will be too late. Trust me, and do what I say!"

Levi hurried outdoors, while Aaron and Acker got into their coats, seized their hats, and quickly followed him. Sabina and the rest of the family, in their wonder at this precipitate proceeding, gathered at the window to see them off, leaving the funeral guests, who crowded in at the door, unheeded until Acker and Aaron had driven away and were out of sight.

"Now, Aaron, we must get to town by some indirect route," Acker explained, "or we may be met by the policemen—and everything depends upon our reaching the undertaker's before they arrest you. What direction shall I take?"

Aaron silently took the reins and turned the mare into a lane. "This here'll take us to the side end of the village near the undertaker's place. What are you thinkin' of doin' at the undertaker's?"

"Drive faster, Aaron. I wish we had your mare instead of this slow old-timer. But if we can avoid *meeting* the policemen on their way out, we're pretty safe. If only we find the undertaker at his place of business!"

"What's *he* to do of it?"

"Aaron! We've all been asses! It was *he* that used the arsenic—to preserve the body. That accounts for the large quantity found by the coroner and me. Why I did not think of it before I don't understand. That's a way the mind has of working—overlooking perfectly obvious facts and searching all around the barn for what's under one's nose. The undertaker must go with us to the justice of the peace and

affirm that he did it—that will end *your* difficulty, and put Mrs. Schwenkfelders' accusations
under your feet."

Aaron tightened the reins and touched
the mare with the whip. "I see through it," he
remarked. "*Yourn* ain't no cabbage-head,
'Gustus!"

The mare answered to the whip and dashed
up the lane at a breakneck pace. In half an hour
they were at the undertaker's house.

"Hurry indoors, Aaron, and leave me to tie
the mare. It isn't safe for you to be seen in town
at this critical time."

Aaron obeyed like a child.

When Acker joined him in the undertaker's
office, the latter was already hearing the story of
the threatened arrest.

"To be sure, it was me used the arsenic, like
what I near always do to preserve a corp'," the
man at once acknowledged. "It didn't never
make me no trouble with no one *before!* I was in
at Lancaster ever since I was out to your place,
Aaron, and I only got home last night, and then
my wife tole me Aaron Wilt should have gave his
wife poison—but it never come to me it was that
there arsenic was meant."

"Aaron should have given his wife poison?"
Acker inquired uncomprehendingly.

"Missus tole me how Mrs. Schwenkfelders should have sayed Aaron he poisoned his wife."

Acker, in his nervousness, felt an unreasoning rage at this senseless distortion of the English tongue.

"Look here," he said sharply, "have you a phone here?"

"To be sure have I."

"Then get a message to that coroner to join us at once at the office of the justice of the peace. Will you go with us, too, right away, to the alderman's office, and swear to the fact of your having used the arsenic? Otherwise Aaron will be arrested this very morning."

"Would Aaron better mebbe hide here till me and you goes alone?" the man suggested.

"I think he had better go with us. If we encounter the police we can persuade them to go with us to the alderman's to hear your oath. But if he were found here alone, they would not listen to his defense of himself."

The three men crowded into the buggy at the door and drove up the village street. The undertaker sat on Aaron's knees and thus hid him from the curious gaze of the villagers, who had begun to hear rumors of the dreadful charge brought against him, and who would have, at any rate, regarded with disapproving

wonder his presence in the street on the day of
his wife's funeral.

At the alderman's office stood the constable's
buggy and another vehicle which, Aaron quickly
told Acker, was Mrs. Schwenkfelders'.

"They will think you have come to give yourself up," Acker said. "We'll give the enemy a
little surprise, won't we?"

"It'll spite Elephena's mom wonderful," murmured Aaron, "that I didn't do it!"

When they entered the office, they were met
by the uncompromising countenance of Mrs.
Schwenkfelders, the stolid face of the constable,
and the self-important, fat little justice of the
peace, who, "dressed in a little brief authority,"
strutted on the stage of life in huge enjoyment
of his prestige among his fellows. The coroner
arrived on the scene almost at the moment of
their entrance.

"Shall we have any trouble with them all?"
Acker wondered a little anxiously.

He summoned all his ingenuity and tact to
meet this combination of feminine spleen, hard-
headed brute force, and ignorant self-esteem.

"So you're come to give yourself up, heh?"
inquired the self-important little squire, his
small keen eyes fixing Aaron as the constable

quickly locked the door to prevent the accused man's escape.

"Thought you'd save me a trip out to the farm, did you?" jocularly inquired the constable. "I was just a-goin' to start."

"It ain't goin' no easier with you fur your comin' to give yourself up!" screamed Mrs. Schwenkfelders, evidently feeling robbed of part of her revenge in not seeing Aaron arrested in his own home and dragged away from the bosom of his family. "You'll *hang* fur this, Aaron Wilt! And I'll be there to see you! You—you—" her emotions choked her so that she could not go on.

"Where's your handcuffs, constable?" the alderman demanded. "You kin take him to Lancaster on the nine-thirty train."

"I got 'em here all righty," the constable answered, shaking the steel rings noisily.

"The undertaker has a little testimony to offer," quietly remarked Acker.

"This here ain't the place or time fur testimony. This here ain't the trial," objected the alderman.

"He merely wishes to state that *he* gave Mrs. Aaron Wilt the arsenic."

The constable's lower lip fell in heavy astonishment. The alderman's little eyes snapped sharply. Mrs. Schwenkfelders' face turned a bit more livid.

"What you givin' us?" the squire demanded authoritatively.

"The undertaker will speak for himself," said Acker, and the man came forward.

"Yes, it was me give her the arsenic. I put it in the corp's stomeek to preserve the body. Like what I do to near all my corp's."

"It ain't so!" shrieked Mrs. Schwenkfelders. "It's a lie got up to save the murderer! This here town dude's a sharper and just smart enough fur them tricks. He's *paid* this here feller to lie about it! He's—"

"Take care, missus," warned the justice of the peace. "You might get sued fur libel if you ain't careful. Go on, Weaver," he addressed the undertaker. "Can you prove me you done it?"

"By my assistant I kin. He was along when I done it. You can phone fur him up and tell him to come down here if you want."

"It ain't necessary," declared the alderman. "This here ain't no case! Aaron Wilt, you're free to go. *You* ain't done it," he said, disgusted at so flat and unprofitable an outcome to what had promised to be the most sensational "case" that had ever come his way. "Missus," he said, addressing Mrs. Schwenkfelders, "you just wanted to make trouble, I guess!"

Mrs. Schwenkfelders' wrath in her defeat found vent in a volley of abuse poured out upon Aaron and Acker. Neither of them paid any attention to her, as they turned at once to leave the office and return to their buggy. The woman's fury passed the bounds of self-restraint, and she made a dash at Aaron as though to clutch his throat. The constable interfered and held her back, and while the alderman was threatening her with arrest, Aaron and Acker left the office.

CHAPTER EIGHTEEN

THE FACE AGAIN

AN AMISH FUNERAL IS AN OCCASION OF A SORT of sad rejoicing, the corpse being quite a secondary consideration to the assembled friends, and the accompanying repast being the principal feature. The funeral of Aaron's wife was to "take up" at one o'clock, but the meal, served at eleven-thirty, lasted so long that the sermon did not begin until nearly two; and Acker was thereby delayed from getting back to town that night.

The next day, when he prepared to return to Lancaster, a hope which he had been persuading himself to cherish during all this trouble of the Wilts was put to flight. It was that, in the shock of grief and fright which Sabina had sustained, her ambition for an education would have received a setback, and that she would now give up her useless struggle at the Normal School, where she was so unhappy and homesick, and remain at home—and ultimately marry Ulmer.

But it was soon borne in upon his consciousness that his having saved her brother had placed him in Sabina's eyes on a pedestal of goodness and cleverness far loftier than her imagination had hitherto elevated him.

"Nothing short of an act of villainy on my part will dissipate the halo she now sees around my head!" he ruefully realized.

Neither the arguments of her family nor the repeated pleadings of the persistent and faithful Ulmer availed to induce her to give up her career at Millersville and stay at home. She would return with Acker on the day after the funeral.

"I'm paid for up to the end of the winter term, and I can't lose all that there," she reasoned, which, of course, was a strong argument on her side to every Amish mind.

"And I kin see the use of book-learnin' now, like I never could before," her father granted. "'Gustus he wouldn't of knew Elephena couldn't of swallered all that there arsenic and kep' it with her if he hadn't been college-learnt. Yes, college-learnt people thinks of things *I* never would think of."

"Och, well," said Aunt Susanna, disparagingly, "I believe in the old sayin', 'A blind hog sometimes finds an acorn, too.' It ain't always college-learnt people that's cute that way."

The next day Acker was once more the escort of Sabina on her journey from New Holland to Millersville.

The gloom of the past week still hanging upon her spirit, she proved a very quiet and pensive traveling-companion, though the gentle radiance of her contentment in his presence was not without its appeal to him. Indeed, when they reached Lancaster, instead of leaving her to take the second half of the trip alone, he decided to go out with her on the Millersville car and see her safe at her school. And it was well that he did so.

"I ain't goin' to leave myself have homesick if I can otherwise help it," Sabina bravely said as they rode toward the place which had been her prison in the saddest hours her young life had known.

"That's right," Acker said approvingly. "Try to make friends with some of the girls, Sabina; go in for a little fun; break the rules now and then!"

Sabina looked at him uncertainly; she did not understand chaffing. "Them's a funny adwice," she said doubtfully, "to tell me to be unconscientious!"

"Oh, you don't know me! Unlike the singed cat, I'm *not* better than I look."

"*What* singed cat?" asked Sabina, wonderingly.

She stopped short, and a sudden clutch upon his arm made him turn quickly. Her eyes, with that strange dilated expression of horror, were fixed upon the opposite end of the car, and her face was livid. Acker followed her gaze and saw the ugly, brutal countenance of a man seated near the door. The man's hair and beard were red, and he had a cut upper lip. His face was pockmarked, and his small eyes were set remarkably close together.

Acker felt a shudder go over him as he instantly recognized in this face the accurate description in every detail which Sabina had given him of her omen of evil. It was unmistakably the Face.

Quickly he placed a protecting hand upon hers.

The man was looking out of the car window and did not appear to be conscious of their staring at him. Sabina's hand quivered under Acker's clasp, but she did not turn to him; her gaze was held as by a serpent's charm.

Suddenly the man slowly turned his carrot-colored head and, apparently for the first time, saw the Amish girl at the other end of the car; for a flash of recognition came into his small close-set eyes. Acker hardly breathed as he watched him.

The man shifted in his seat, and his eyes narrowed to a concentrated gaze upon Sabina. His stare was not bold, but furtive and embarrassed; and a self-conscious look stole over his countenance like that of a small bad boy unexpectedly caught in some mischief.

Acker became suddenly aware that Sabina's hand which he held under his own had become cold. Turning to look at her, he was startled to find that she was deathly white, that her breath was coming in faint gasps, and that she seemed on the verge of losing consciousness.

Instantly he signaled to stop the car, realizing that she must be removed at once from this fatal presence, or the effect on her already shattered nerves might be disastrous. "We will get off here, Sabina," he whispered close to her ear. "Let me help you."

She made an effort to rally from her half faint, and allowed him to take her arm and support her out of the car.

As he stood holding her up in the road while the car moved on, his anxiety for her was mixed with a regret that he had been obliged to allow the man to escape from him.

The cold air and her removal from the menace of that face of ill omen quickly revived the fainting girl. But Acker saw that she had received a frightful shock and that her condition was serious.

"We are only five minutes' walk from the school, Sabina," he gently encouraged her. "Can you manage to walk? Or we can sit down on this pile of logs and wait until a wagon or carriage comes along to give us a lift."

"I'll try to walk," she answered feebly. "I'll mebbe feel better to be movin'."

She could scarcely speak, and when they started down the road he bore her weight almost to the extent of carrying her.

He soothed and encouraged her as though she were a sick child, but she was able to answer his kindness only with the grateful glance of her eyes. She looked as though she had received a mortal blow, and Acker was genuinely alarmed about her.

He managed, however, to get her to the school and put her into the preceptress' charge; and when he had left her, with the assurance that he would see her again very soon, he went at once to the office of the principal and told him the whole story.

"Now," he asked in conclusion, as the two men, seated on either side of the professor's office table, leaned toward each other in earnest consultation, "how am I to go about finding that man? He must be somewhere in this village at this minute, for the car doesn't go beyond Millersville."

"Unless he went back with it to Lancaster," the professor suggested. "He may not wish to encounter any friends of the girl. That is to say, *if*—"

"Well? If?"

"If the whole thing isn't a delusion. The man's resemblance to the face described by the girl may be a mere coincidence."

"I would think so," Acker granted, "but for the unmistakable flash of recognition when he saw her this afternoon on the car, and his look of self-conscious, guilty embarrassment."

"What do you expect to get out of him?"

"I haven't the least idea. Naturally, however, I want to investigate him."

"Do you really believe that that fellow has anything to do with the premonitions this girl has had?" the professor skeptically asked.

"I'm open to conviction," Acker affirmed. "The thing is incomprehensible, of course—perhaps impossible. I don't know—I want to find out."

"I confess your story has excited my interest. I'll keep a lookout in the village and collar the fellow if I see him."

"Thank you."

With promises from both the preceptress and the principal that he should have daily telephone messages of Sabina's condition until she was quite herself again, and the principal's further assurance that he should hear from him at once if he saw or learned anything of the mysterious red-headed man, Acker left the school and went back to the city of Lancaster.

Next day Acker determined that he would call up the school immediately after breakfast and inquire how Sabina was; for he found himself haunted by an inexplicable something which, when he had left her the day before, had seemed to stamp the girl's aspect. He could not define just what it was, but it gave him a vague uneasiness in the thought of her which he could not put aside.

While he was at breakfast, however, the bell called him to the telephone, and he felt intuitively that the message was from Millersville.

"This is Mr. Acker?" came the principal's voice in response to his "Hello!"

"Yes. This is the office of the Normal School?" inquired Acker.

"Yes. Miss Wilt is seriously ill. Her fever is high and she is delirious. The doctor fears brain-fever. We have sent word to her parents, and we have been obliged to employ a nurse for her. She is too ill to be removed to a hospital. She keeps raving about that 'face.'"

Acker thanked him for calling him up and begged to be informed of any changes in the girl's condition.

"Is there anything I can do either here or in town or by coming out to the school?" he inquired.

"No; every possible thing is being done," he was told.

He felt his work unspeakably irksome that morning. His mind was so wholly taken up with the illness and suffering of the tormented girl, in whose experiences he felt a deep and anxious interest.

"She will die!" he grimly told himself as he paced his studio floor. "I know it. She will never get over this. She said that if she ever saw that face again she would go crazy or die. And to see it in the flesh! Poor, poor girl!"

Oddly mixed with his keen pain in this conviction, which bore so heavily upon him, was his scientific interest in solving the problem of the possible connection between Sabina's illness and the red-haired man. *Was* there any real connection? Was that low-browed, animal-like specimen of humanity capable of projecting the psychic part of himself at will to touch and torment the spirit of another? Could such things be? That Sabina was a good "psychic subject" he could not question. He had had proof enough of that to convince the most skeptical.

When at the end of the long morning he sat at his luncheon, he realized that, running through all his speculations and emotions, there had been, all morning, an undercurrent of quite practical appreciation of the consternation the Wilts would feel at the expense of this illness of Sabina's. To be obliged to pay for a nurse's hire and for her board at the school would be nothing short of tragic to Levi. Acker knew that not even their alarm and distress at their daughter's danger would modify their pain in parting with their hoarded dollars for such unwonted expenditure.

This impression was quite confirmed when on the next day he met Levi and Naomi at the New Holland car and transferred them to the car for Millersville. News had come from the school that Sabina was critically ill with brain-fever, her temperature having steadily gone up.

"It'll cost expensive, her havin' so sick there instead of at her home, where we could take care of her," Naomi lamented.

"When will you go home again?" he inquired of them. "I'll meet you here if you will telephone me what car you will take."

"We're got to be home till tonight a'ready," Levi answered. "Naomi she'd like to stay with Biney till she's well onct; but she won't stay with all them strangers without I stay too. And, to be sure, that I can't do."

"Sabina is delirious and won't know you, and her illness is so serious that she requires the care of an experienced nurse," Acker told them; "so that there is no real necessity for your remaining."

"It's wonderful the trouble we're havin' this while back, ain't?" Naomi plaintively said.

"You are having your share, certainly," Acker gravely answered. "How is Aaron?"

"He's tryin' to rent his place so's he can come home ag'in. He says he can't stand it fur to stay there and see poor Elephena's empty chair at the table. Aunt Susanna she's cookin' fur him till he can rent onct. I had to take all the children over and let 'em at Aaron's today when we come away."

"Does Mrs. Schwenkfelders give you any more annoyance?"

"The Lord's punishin' her fur her bad heart," answered Levi. "She's took with heart disease wonderful bad and is failin' rapid."

At nine o'clock that night Acker met the quaint pair once more in the square on their return trip. They were both very white and worn with the strain of the day's hard experience. He was told that poor Biney "had wonderful sick" and the doctor would not be able to tell for several days whether or not she would get well; and they had to pay four dollars a week for the nurse's board at the school and a dollar a day for her work in taking care of Biney.

Two days passed by, during which the reports of the sick girl's condition left her recovery in grave doubt. And then, on the next night, at about ten o'clock, Acker was called to the telephone by the Millersville principal.

"I have seen the red-haired man!" was the message which greeted him.

"Have you got hold of him?"

"No; but three times today I have seen that man walk by the grounds of this school."

"Well?" Acker tensely inquired.

"And Miss Wilt has been more delirious today than at any time since her illness. Her fever is up to a hundred and four."

"You are absolutely sure it was the man?"

"I can't be mistaken. Red hair and beard, a cut upper lip, and a pockmarked face. I recognized him at once; he had the bearing of a sneak-thief—a most suspicious-looking cur! I saw him the first time from my office window. The second time I was just starting off on the car to Lancaster. The third time was at nightfall, and I was strolling in the grounds. Twice I made an effort to get at him, but he was off before I could reach him."

"I'll come out to Millersville tomorrow to find him," Acker affirmed.

"He may not come near the place again. And without the least clue as to his name or his whereabouts, what steps could you take to find him?"

"Can't something be done?"

"I shall have two men on the watch for him— one here in our grounds and another in the village. If he is about again, he will be found. I have become as much interested as you are in solving this thing."

"And Miss Wilt? Is there any hope?"

"Tonight must settle it one way or the other, the doctor says. The fever *must* be broken tonight, or she will die. If she live until morning, she will probably get well, unless she is too exhausted to rally. In that case she may linger a few days."

"You will telephone me in the morning?"

"As soon as there is any change," was the reply.

There was little or no sleep for Acker that night. He fully believed that Sabina would die before dawn.

Very early next morning he arose, his anxiety making it impossible for him to remain in bed.

It was hard to resist the temptation to anticipate the promised telephone summons from the Millersville principal and call him up at daybreak. The hours of waiting for the message from the school seemed endless. Acker walked the floor while he watched the slow-moving hands of the clock. He ate no breakfast, taking only a cup of strong coffee because he felt he needed a stimulant.

Eight o'clock came, and the telephone bell had not called him. What could cause the delay? No news ought to be good news, surely. But the crisis must long since have passed. Why was he not informed? He controlled his suspense and determined not to annoy the principal by calling him—for another half-hour at least. But shortly before half-past eight his long wait was brought to an end.

"I have kept you waiting," the principal's voice spoke. "I had to go to town to the market this morning. I have only just got back."

"Yes," Acker prompted, a little impatiently.

"Before I left, Sabina was still in a critical condition, with high fever and delirium."

"And now?"

"It was too early, then, to phone you—I thought you wouldn't be up—and the doctor advised me to wait until I got back."

"There is now a change for the better?" Acker hurried his story.

"On my way to town, our trolley car had to wait at King Street for a train to pass. At one of the windows of that train, bound for Reading, I suppose, I distinctly saw our red-haired, pock-marked friend. So you see he has escaped us."

"Well?"

"It was about seven o'clock when his train passed out of the town. The doctor assures me that at seven o'clock Sabina's delirium suddenly left her and she fell asleep."

"And now?" Acker repeated patiently.

"The fever is broken, and the doctor has strong hopes of her recovery."

Acker's relief was so great that for the time being he paid no attention to the fact that the solution of the mystery which hung about

Sabina had been lost, probably, in the departure of the man with the haunting, evil face.

The reaction he experienced from the tension of the night left him weak and exhausted all that day.

CHAPTER NINETEEN

ULMER MAKES A DISCOVERY

"SAY, BINEY!"

Sabina turned languidly from the kitchen window, at which she sat in a rocking chair, a pillow at her back and a stool at her feet, and looked at her Aunt Susanna inquiringly. She was convalescing, now, at home, and her pallor, the short curls which were growing all over her head, which had been shaven, and the wonderful light in her large dark eyes, gave a new and more spiritual beauty to her pensive face. It was five o'clock on a December evening, just after supper, and she and Aunt Susanna were alone in the kitchen, the latter washing the dishes at the sink.

"Well, what?" Biney asked, a note of weariness in her soft voice.

"Say, Biney," Aunt Susanna repeated hesitatingly, keeping her eyes on the dishpan and not venturing to look at the girl, for she was about to tread on dangerous ground in order to discover that which Biney's physician had forbidden to be mentioned to her. "Say, I was a-goin' to ast you onct, is Ulmer comin' to keep comp'ny with you this evening?"

"If Ulmer's comin'?" Sabina dully repeated. "I guess maybe. I don't know."

"A body'd think you'd take interest a little, Biney, in your own friend! Are you mebbe thinkin' about—about that other party?" Aunt Susanna put out tentatively.

Sabina lifted her drowsy eyes questioningly to her aunt's face.

"What other party?"

"You know who I mean, Biney Wilt."

Biney appeared to consider the matter for a moment and then to give it up wearily.

"Say, Aunt Susanna," she said fretfully, "this here pear tree by the window she so shuts the road from sight. I'm goin' to ast pop to have her cut down onct—she comes me so in the eyes. And when it has windy weather out, she so noisy!"

"Ach, Biney, you're got it so in your nerves since you had so sick! Mebbe," Aunt Susanna ventured another experimental query, "you don't like the pear tree to shut the road out because you're lookin' fur someone comin'?"

230 SABINA: A STORY OF THE AMISH

"Ulmer comes by the lane over, not the road."

"But mebbe it ain't Ulmer."

Sabina looked mystified for a moment, then giving it up with a sigh, turned her eyes again to the window.

It was perhaps an hour later when the family, assembled in the kitchen for a little while before going to bed, heard a buggy come up through the back gate.

"It's Ulmer, likely, come to keep comp'ny with Biney again this Saturday," remarked Naomi. "Ain't, Biney?"

"I guess," Biney nodded, without turning her eyes from the window beside which she still sat.

Aunt Susanna hastily set down the lamp she was about to light to go upstairs, and slipped out at the back door.

"What does Aunt Susanna want with speakin' to aside with Ulmer, I wonder," said Naomi, as she rose to collect the children and convey them to the inner chamber of the first floor.

Biney did not answer. Her mother went away with the children, and her father and Aaron silently followed suit, the latter going heavily upstairs to his own bedroom.

"Ach, Ulmer," Aunt Susanna was meantime greeting the faithful lover as he tied his horse at the back porch, "I ain't got nothin' out of her, fur all I pumped wonderful!"

"Couldn't you get her to speak nothin'?" Ulmer asked, coming to Aunt Susanna's side and speaking low.

"Nothin' that I could put two and two together by."

"But couldn't you tell nothin' at her face if she cares fur that feller yet?"

"If I sayed I could, Ulmer, I wouldn't be spea-kin' what's right. You'll have to find out fur yourself, Ulmer."

Thus goaded, if not encouraged, to his task, Ulmer entered the house and joined Sabina at the kitchen window. It was his third visit to her since she had been well enough to see anyone outside her own family.

Now, the doctor had forbidden the mention of any distressing subject to Sabina until she had entirely regained her strength. But Ulmer, impatient to know how he stood in her affec-tions, and unable to find out without some reference to persons—or a person—associated with the recent painful episodes in the Wilt household, was in a quandary as to his course. He had determined, during his ride over to the Wilt farm tonight, that he would not go home without ascertaining, even at the risk of exciting

Biney a little, whether or not she was still "gone on that dude."

The only reason he had for thinking that perhaps everything was over between her and Acker was that the artist had not been near her since she had been brought home.

The family left the two alone in the kitchen, and at nine o'clock, according to the local method of courting, Ulmer turned out the light and sat with Biney in the darkness, his arm about her waist, her hand held in his.

"It's nice out this evening, say not, Ulmer?" Biney said softly.

"Yes. It ain't so cold like this morning. I like the wintertime best. You can make to keep warm in the wintertime, but you can't make to keep cool in summer."

"That's so, too," Sabina agreed.

"Ain't you got the thick hairs now, Biney!" Ulmer remarked, as his fingers clumsily smoothed the wilful curls on her forehead.

"Yes, but they get so in the eyes. I'd keep 'em brushed back under my cap, still, accordin' to the rules of Meetin', if I otherwise could."

"They're wain, but they're—they're—well, it ain't fur us Amish to consider such things, but I can't help fur it—I think they're *pretty*, Biney. I could a'most wish our Amish females addicted to such. . . . You won't never feel fur goin' back to that there Millersville Normal again, will you?" he asked suddenly, while his heart beat fast.

In the darkness he could not see, in the expression of her face, how she took his question.

"What you talkin', Ulmer? You speak as if *I* ever went to the Normal."

"Well, to be sure it was only fur a little while. But yet you *went*."

"When did I?" Sabina demanded combatively.

"Why," Ulmer said in surprise, "there, last September."

"*Me?*" exclaimed Biney. "Why, Ulmer Popple! You know I didn't, neither! What would *I* want with that there education, and me an Amish girl!"

"Well, Biney, didn't you go to the Millersville Normal there fur a couple months?"

"I don't know what you want to make such jokes fur, Ulmer. I don't think they're comic."

"Didn't you go to the Normal in with that there 'Gustus Acker from Lancaster?"

For a moment Biney was silent.

"Ulmer," she presently answered in a bored tone, "you was misinformed. I ain't acquainted with no sich a party from the city. And I never

even have saw the Millersville Normal. Who
spoke you such things about me, Ulmer? Was
Barbara Schnabel talkin' down on me to you?"

"Why, but, Biney," the bewildered Ulmer
exclaimed, "you know yous had a boarder last
August here—'Gustus Acker!"

Again Sabina was silent for a moment.

"Ulmer," she presently said in a distressed
voice, "I don't mind nothin' about last August.
It's like as if there hadn't been no last August. I
can't seem to think back. I guess I had wonderful sick fur a long time, ain't?"

"You wasn't took sick till near November
a'ready. Do you want to tell me, Biney," he
asked incredulously, "you don't mind last August
and—'Gustus Acker?"

"No, I don't mind him. Who's *him?*"

Ulmer was silent from sheer bewilderment.
Neither of them spoke for several minutes.
Sabina was the first to break the painful tension.

"Ulmer," she said tentatively.

For answer he again took her hand in his.

"Do you ever see Elephena up your way?"

She asked the question with an accent of
anxiety.

Ulmer's clasp of her hand tightened spas-
modically. "Why, Biney!" he faltered. "Elephena?
What you speakin'?"

"She don't never come here no more, Ulmer. Does she ever get up your way?"

"No," he stammered, "not just to say up *our* way."

"Aaron he looks downhearted and don't say nothin' about her. I started to speak somepin' about her to mom and pop and Aunt Susanna, but they sayed I wasn't enough strong to talk about Elephena yet."

"So you ain't, Biney," he murmured.

"But I want you to tell me what's the matter of her, if you know. Did her and Aaron break it off?"

Ulmer, mindful, in his confusion, of the doctor's warning that Biney must not be excited on these painful themes, made a staggering attempt to answer judiciously. "Well, in one way you look at it—yes."

"Does she take it as downhearted as Aaron does, I wonder? How is she now, Ulmer?"

"How she is now? Well—she's—she's still dead, Biney."

"What?" breathed Biney, sitting upright. "What d'you say?"

"Elephena she died," he affirmed, "and she's dead."

Biney sank back again among her cushions with a little gasp. "Did she die while I had so sick?"

"Before that."

"*Before?*"

"Yes."

"What did she die of?"

"Of her heart failin' her."

"Oh! And *that's* why I ain't seen her round, and why Aaron he's so downhearted."

"Yes."

Sabina drew a long, deep breath and considered the news in silence.

"Biney!"

"Well, what, Ulmer?"

"What's the last you mind of before you had sick?"

"Me and you was goin' in town circus day. But I don't mind if we went. I can't think back no furder than the week before that there time we was goin' in on circus day. I mind I wrestled with the Enemy's temptin' me to say to you that now I'd like onct to look at a circus parade, if you'd go along too and look."

Ulmer's heart beat thick in his breast. Two years of her life burned out of Sabina's memory by that terrible fever! Even the very memory of "that dude" "clean gone" from her! How strange and wonderful! To have forgotten entirely the very existence of his rival! Ulmer could hardly credit it that such good fortune had befallen him in his long-suffering courtship. But could it possibly continue—this strange oblivion of what had meant so much in her life? Would she not presently recall all that was now a blank? He passionately hoped that she would not!

He realized that if she did not remember their having seen the circus, she, no doubt, did not remember that haunting Face that had caused her so much misery. What a good thing it was if that was forgotten!

He wondered a little at the fact that the Wilts had not yet discovered Sabina's loss of memory. How amazed and how relieved they all would be!

He remembered that two years ago, about the time of that circus day in town, Biney had been much more favorably disposed to him than she had been recently. So he took heart to hope from this fact that she would hear him favorably now.

He smoothed her hand and hugged her soft, yielding body up to his side in a deep contentment of relief and love, for these familiarities do not wait upon a betrothal among the Pennsylvania Germans.

"Biney," he begged, "leave us get published in Meeting as soon as we otherwise can make it suit; ain't you will?"

"It's all the same to me, Ulmer. If you want."
She expressed herself with maidenly reserve. "It
has to be did *sometime*. We might as well have
it over and done with."

"Then as soon as you're enough strong,
Biney!" the lover ardently urged.

"It's all the same to me," she repeated.

As Ulmer wended his joyful and triumphant
way home that night, there was mingled with
his innocent happiness a rather ghoulish exul-
tation in his contemplation of the enjoyment
he would have in telling "'Gustus" Acker, if he
ever had an opportunity, that the girl he had
tried to beguile away from her rightful lover
didn't even remember his existence. The fearful possibility that presently everything would
come back to her, he resolutely kept in the
background of his consciousness.

CHAPTER TWENTY

Epilogue

It was a hot afternoon at the end of June. Augustus Acker had taken off his coat and was carrying it over his arm as he trudged along the country road from New Holland to the Wilt farm.

He found himself contemplating with some wonder his own state of mind and emotion. It was two years since he had last been over this road; two years since he had seen the Amish maiden, Biney Wilt. His art studies in Paris, which had occupied his best thought and effort during all that time, had never for one day blotted from his mind the image that always dwelt there, persistently haunting him with its indefinable charm—the image of Biney.

He had not yet painted the great picture which was to reveal that fascinating image to the world. He must see her once more before he dared to enter upon the task into which he knew he would put the best of which he was capable.

He had wondered sometimes during these two years whether, if he could have found the man of the haunting face, and perhaps learned through him some explanation of Sabina's premonitions, he would not then have been able more easily to throw off the spell in which his memory of the girl had held him all this time. But the man had eluded his search and inquiries, and the mystery of Sabina had remained unsolved.

That Sabina's mind was a blank as to all that had happened in the memorable weeks preceding her illness he had learned from the Wilts. But there were many questions he wanted to ask and one he almost dreaded to have answered. Was Biney married to Ulmer? Had the memory of him ever come back to her? If so, had it come before or after her marriage, and had the return of her memory brought with it her old feeling for him? Now that he was near to hearing the answers to these questions which for two long years had haunted every conscious hour of his life, he found himself strangely agitated.

"I ought not to be going out here today," he told himself, as with long strides he toiled along the dusty road. "Why do I dally with fire like this? When one has been burned one keeps away from the flame. What is it going to do for me—my seeing Biney again, even though she does not remember me?"

There was a half-defined hope in his mind that this pilgrimage to New Holland would dispel his own illusion as to the girl's charm, and that he would thus rid himself of the haunting image that had so unsettled him in his work.

"Surely I've been idealizing her, and this creature of my fancy has no real existence outside my imagination! When I see her again I shall no doubt wonder at my absurd infatuation. I shall probably find her grown stout and coarse. Very well. All the better."

Aunt Susanna was the first of the family to meet him. She was hanging the Saturday's clean roller-towel on the back porch as he opened the gate and came around to the kitchen. Her mingled astonishment, curiosity, pleasure, and, of course, apprehension at sight of him gave him a sense of the renewal of an old sensation of glee in her idiosyncrasies that in itself was sufficient compensation for this hot tramp from New Holland.

"Well, now, to think! Who'd of thought to see you so unexpected! If it wasn't only this wery day I was speakin' somepin' to Naomi about you! I sayed to her I wondered was you married and settled yet and leavin' off your wanderin's about the world, I sayed. Yes, only this morning yet! Now mind if I wasn't! There's a sayin', 'When we speak about an ass he will come.' And so you come, ain't? Don't it, now, beat all! What brang you anyhow? And are you still wanderin' to and fro up and down the earth? Ain't you never found no woman yet to suit you?"

"I've heeded your warnings, Aunt Susanna: 'Happy who is single yet, sad who is engaged.' How is everybody here?"

"Well, come in and set, and I'll tell you," she said hospitably, leading the way into the kitchen. "Us we're all pretty good just now. Aaron he had it so bad in his head there fur a while—he'd have the headache near every night. But he overgrowed it till spring. Then Naomi she took the cold, and I thought it would give consumption. Yes, indeed, she had a wonderful cough. But Levi he fetched a bottle of cough-mixture along out from Lancaster, and till it was near all, a'ready, she'd outgrowed her cough. Me I had it so in my back—"

"And Sabina?" Acker gently interrupted, unable longer to endure his suspense. He seated himself at the kitchen table, white from its Saturday's scrubbing.

"She's pretty good again," Aunt Susanna reluctantly granted; it always hurt her to concede good health to anyone. "I'm sorry, 'Gustus, that they're all off this after. Naomi she went with Levi to Lancaster in, this morning, when he went to market, because she wanted to buy some calico onct. Aaron and Sammy they're in the field out, and Melinda and Sarah they went with Naomi and Levi along."

"Does Sabina—did she—has she ever—did she ever recall all that she had forgotten?"

"No. She don't mind nothin'. Leastways, she ain't never spoke about them things. She never said nothin' about you—or the Face—or the Normal. We don't never mind her of them. The doctor says best not to."

"Is she—at home?"

"Yes, so far as I know."

"May I see her? Or do you think it better that I should not?"

"I don't know. Better mebbe not to. It might bring things up where she's better to have overgrowed. 'What we know not, hurts us not,' the sayin' goes."

"In that case—you say she's at home—must I leave at once?"

"Och, I meant she's over to her own home."

"Her own home? Sabina is—married?"

"Och, this long time a'ready. Her and Ulmer they got married as soon as Biney was otherwise able to. They live up the road a piece."

Acker did not speak. He stared at Aunt Susanna absently.

"She's fixed nice, too. I wisht you could walk over and see her place. But I guess mebbe you hadn't better ought."

"Is Sabina happy?"

"Whether she's happy?" Aunt Susanna repeated vaguely. It was a question too searching for the average Amish intellect. "I never ast her if she *is* or no. I guess mebbe she is. She ain't never said nothin'. She ain't got nothin' to bother her much. To be sure, her first baby's cuttin' his stomeek-teeth and—"

"She has children?"

"Yes, a boy a year old and a girl two month."

Again Acker gazed at Aunt Susanna with unseeing eyes.

"I wonder if she *would* mind of you if she seen you," Aunt Susanna speculated.

As though in confirmation of one of her pet proverbs, the kitchen door was at this moment pushed open, and Sabina herself walked into the room.

Acker made a movement to rise; yet somehow he could not. He sat spellbound, gazing at her.

She stopped half-way across the room as her eyes fell upon the stranger. Acker became conscious of the new and subtle beauty of her riper womanhood—the more rounded cheek, the fuller bosom, the softer curve of the lips, the more mellow countenance.

She looked inquiringly at her aunt.

"This here's a friend of your mom's and pop's, Biney"—Aunt Susanna presented him with self-conscious diplomacy—"by name 'Gustus Acker."

Biney looked at him shyly from under her dark-blue bonnet. He rose and held out his hand, and she limply offered her own.

"Did you fetch the babies with, Biney?" Aunt Susanna inquired.

"Yes; they're both sleepin' out on the porch in the baby carriage."

Her eyes returned to Acker as he went back to his chair by the table.

"Does little Ulmer fret much today by his cuttin' his teeth?"

"Wonderful much," Biney nodded.

"Why don't you set?" demanded her aunt.

Biney did not answer. She was gazing at Acker.

Aunt Susanna pushed a chair toward her. "You must be some tired pushin' a heavy baby-coach through the dust."

Biney took no heed of the chair. She stood transfixed, looking at the visitor.

"Biney!" exclaimed Aunt Susanna, uneasily. "What makes you act so dumm?"

With a fast-beating heart, Acker saw a strange glint coming into Biney's eyes—the clairvoyant look that had baffled and puzzled him in his first acquaintance with her.

Suddenly she turned white and began to tremble.

She started toward him, the light of recognition slowly dawning in her eyes.

"Why, it's you—why, it's—" she paused, trying desperately to remember.

Then sharp and clear came the wailing cry of an infant, that presently trailed off into a hungry whimper.

The magic of that cry! It broke the spell that held her. All bewilderment and terror fled from the girl's features. For a moment she stood listening, her head half turned to the porch, her eyes still on Acker's face. And again came that appealing cry; and Sabina flew to her baby. Acker slowly followed, and watched her as she picked it up and crooned over it, too absorbed in it, and its need of her, to notice him further.

When, a few minutes later, he said good-by, she glanced over her shoulder to watch him go slowly down the road. She frowned slightly, a puzzled look in the dark eyes, which presently softened with infinite love and tenderness as she turned to her babies again.